**The route to your**

When they look back at their formative years, many Indians nostalgically recall the vital part Amar Chitra Katha picture books have played in their lives. It was **ACK – Amar Chitra Katha** – that first gave them a glimpse of their glorious heritage.

Since they were introduced in 1967, there are now **over 400 Amar Chitra Katha** titles to choose from. **Over 90 million copies** have been sold worldwide.

Now the Amar Chitra Katha titles are even more widely available in **1000+ bookstores all across India**. Log on to www.ack-media.com to locate a bookstore near you. If you do not have access to a bookstore, you can buy all the titles through our online store **www.amarchitrakatha.com**. We provide quick delivery anywhere in the world.

To make it easy for you to locate the titles of your choice from our treasure trove of titles, the books are now arranged in five categories.

### Epics and Mythology
Best known stories from the Epics and the Puranas

### Indian Classics
Enchanting tales from Indian literature

### Fables and Humour
Evergreen folktales, legends and tales of wisdom and humour

### Bravehearts
Stirring tales of brave men and women of India

### Visionaries
Inspiring tales of thinkers, social reformers and nation builders

## Amar Chitra Katha Pvt Ltd

© Amar Chitra Katha Pvt Ltd, 2000, Reprinted September 2011, ISBN 81-89999-82-6
Published & Printed by Amar Chitra Katha Pvt. Ltd., The Forum, 3rd Floor,
Raghuvanshi Mill Compound, S.B.Marg, Lower Parel (W), Mumbai- 400 013. India

**The route to your roots**

# BUDDHA

King Suddhodana was at his wit's end. He had surrounded his handsome young heir with comfort and riches, love and respect, but Prince Siddhartha was still not content. One night, the prince abandoned his family. Exchanging his royal robes for a begging bowl, his luxurious palace for the shade of a tree, Siddhartha lived the life of an ascetic to seek the ultimate truth about life and suffering. His search led him to enlightenment and he became Buddha - the Awakened One.

**Script**
S.K. Ramachandra

**Illustrations**
Souren Roy

**Editor**
Anant Pai

Cover illustration by: P. D. Chopra

IN THE HIMALAYAN FOOTHILLS, KAPILAVASTU WAS A SMALL BUT PROSPEROUS KINGDOM. THE SAKYAS RULED OVER IT. SUDDHODANA WAS THEIR KING.

ONE DAY, HIS QUEEN, MAYA-DEVI, DREAMT THAT A WHITE ELEPHANT WITH SIX TUSKS, PIERCED HER WOMB.

TEN MONTHS LATER THE QUEEN WAS ON HER WAY TO HER FATHER'S HOUSE. AS SHE WAS PASSING THROUGH A BEAUTIFUL GROVE ON THE WAY TO LUMBINI—

STOP! I WOULD LIKE TO SPEND SOME TIME HERE.

THE QUEEN GOT DOWN AND STARTED WALKING TOWARDS A SALA TREE IN THE MIDDLE OF THE GARDEN. SUDDENLY—

I AM IN GREAT PAIN. I MUST REST.

THERE A BABY WAS BORN TO HER. IT WAS THE FULL MOON NIGHT OF VAISAKHA. THERE WAS SILENCE ALL AROUND.

ON HEARING THE NEWS, THE KING RUSHED TO LUMBINI AND BROUGHT THE MOTHER AND THE CHILD TO THE PALACE. SAGE ASITA CAME TO THE PALACE TO SEE THE BABY.

I SEE TEARS IN YOUR EYES, SAGE ASITA. WHY ARE YOU UNHAPPY?

THIS BOY WILL BE A KING OF KINGS...OR A GREAT SAINT. I AM CRYING BECAUSE I WILL NOT LIVE TO HEAR HIS GREAT WORDS.

BOTH THE KING AND THE QUEEN WERE HAPPY. ON THE FIFTH DAY—

LET US NAME HIM SIDDHARTHA.

AND WE WILL SEE THAT HE BECOMES A KING OF KINGS AND NOT A SAINT.

IMMEDIATELY AFTERWARDS THE QUEEN BECAME SERIOUSLY ILL.

ON THE SEVENTH DAY AFTER THE BIRTH OF SIDDHARTHA—

SISTER PRAJAPATI, I SHALL SOON LEAVE THIS WORLD. WHEN I AM GONE, PLEASE BE A KIND MOTHER TO SIDDHARTHA. PROMISE ME.

I PROMISE.

AFTER A YEAR HAD PASSED—

YOU HAVE BEEN A GOOD MOTHER TO HIM, PRAJAPATI.

I LOVE HIM DEARLY. I AM PROUD TO BE HIS MOTHER.

AS SIDDHARTHA GREW, THE KING BECAME ANXIOUS ABOUT THE PROPHECY.

HE SPENDS SO MUCH TIME ALONE, UNDER THAT JAMBU TREE. I DON'T LIKE THAT.

HE SAYS, HIS PLAYMATES PLAY CRUEL GAMES.

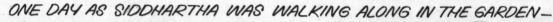

ONE DAY AS SIDDHARTHA WAS WALKING ALONG IN THE GARDEN—

POOR BIRD! I WONDER WHOSE ARROW HAS HURT HIM.

SIDDHARTHA GENTLY REMOVED THE ARROW AND TENDED TO THE BIRD'S WOUND. SOME TIME LATER—

THIS IS MY BIRD. I SHOT IT! GIVE IT TO ME.

IT WAS DEVADATTA, SIDDHARTHA'S COUSIN.

DEVADATTA! IT IS SUCH A LOVELY BIRD. WHY DO YOU WISH TO HARM IT?

THE BIRD BE-LONGS TO ME. GIVE IT BACK.

I WON'T DO THAT.

THE MATTER WAS TAKEN TO THE COURT—

PRINCE! WHAT RIGHT HAVE YOU TO KEEP THE BIRD?

SIR, IF I HAD NOT REMOVED THE ARROW, THE BIRD WOULD HAVE DIED. THE BIRD OWES ITS LIFE TO ME. SHOULD THE BIRD BELONG TO THE ONE WHO TOOK ITS LIFE OR TO THE ONE WHO GAVE IT LIFE?

WHAT THE BOY SAYS IS RIGHT. THE ONE WHO SAVED THE LIFE OF THE BIRD HAS A GREATER RIGHT. DEVADATTA, THE BIRD BELONGS TO THE PRINCE.

THANK YOU, NOBLE JUDGES.

YEARS ROLLED BY. DANDAPANI, A SAKYAN NOBLE ARRANGED THE SWAYAMVARA OF HIS DAUGHTER, YASHODHARA. PRINCES FROM FAR AND NEAR CAME TO THE SWAYAMVARA.

YASHODHARA CHOSE SIDDHARTHA AS HER HUSBAND.

6

THE ASSEMBLED PRINCES WERE HURT BY YASHODHARA'S CHOICE. THEY APPROACHED DANDAPANI.

SIR THE PRINCESS SHOULD NOT BE MARRIED TO SIDDHARTHA. HE IS NOT A GOOD FIGHTER.

SIR, YOU SHOULD HOLD A TEST IN ARCHERY. THE PRINCESS SHOULD BE GIVEN IN MARRIAGE TO THE WINNER.

DANDAPANI TRIED TO PERSUADE HIS DAUGHTER.

YASHODHARA! CHOOSE SOMEONE ELSE AS YOUR HUSBAND.

FATHER, I HAVE MADE MY CHOICE. PLEASE AGREE TO IT.

WHEN THE NEWS REACHED KING SUDDHODANA, HE FELT SAD.

FATHER, WHY ARE YOU SAD?

THE PEOPLE DON'T THINK YOU ARE A GOOD WARRIOR.

FATHER, LET DANDAPANI HOLD A TEST. I WILL TAKE PART IN IT.

I AM HAPPY TO HEAR THAT. YOUR ANCESTORS WERE GREAT WARRIORS, SIDDHARTHA.

MANY GATHERED TO WITNESS THE TEST.

IT IS SIDDHARTHA WHO HAS WON IN HORSE-RIDING.

NO ONE COULD EQUAL HIM IN ARCHERY TOO!

SIDDHARTHA AND YASHODHARA WERE MARRIED WITH GREAT POMP.

THE KING TRIED HIS BEST TO PROVIDE ALL THE COMFORTS OF LIFE TO SIDDHARTHA.

SOON, A SON WAS BORN TO THEM. KING SUDDHODANA WAS PLEASED WHEN HE HEARD THE NEWS.

LORD! IT IS A BOY!

GOOD! NOW SIDDHARTHA WILL NEVER THINK OF BECOMING A SAINT.

ONE DAY_

FATHER, I WOULD LIKE TO GO OUT OF THE PALACE AND SEE MORE OF THE WORLD.

I WILL ORDER A CHARIOT FOR YOU. AFTER IT IS READY, YOU CAN GO OUT IN IT.

A FEW DAYS LATER, IN A BEAUTIFUL CHARIOT WITH FOUR HORSES DRIVEN BY CHANNA, SIDDHARTHA DROVE THROUGH THE STREETS OF THE CITY.

HOW HANDSOME THE PRINCE IS.

I HAVE HEARD, HE IS BRAVE AND FEARLESS.

IN THE CITY, KING SUDDHODANA HAD ORDERED ALL SIGHTS OF UNHAPPINESS TO BE KEPT AWAY FROM SIDDHARTHA. BUT AS HE DROVE FURTHER—

CHANNA, WHO IS THIS? HIS HEAD IS WHITE. HE SEEMS VERY WEAK. HIS SKIN IS WRINKLED.

HE IS AN OLD MAN, MASTER! HE IS BENT WITH AGE.

DOES EVERYONE GET OLD, CHANNA?

YES, MY LORD! EVERYONE HAS TO GROW OLD.

WILL MY YASHODHARA ALSO GROW OLD? WILL MY STRENGTH GO AWAY WITH YEARS?

ON ANOTHER DAY—

WHAT IS THE MATTER WITH THIS MAN?

HE IS ILL, MY LORD! HE IS CRYING WITH PAIN.

IS DISEASE PECULIAR TO HIM?

NO, MY LORD! ANYONE MAY FALL ILL IN HIS LIFETIME.

EVEN I?

YES, MASTER, EVEN YOU.

*STILL ANOTHER DAY—*
WHY ARE THEY CARRYING THAT MAN, CHANNA?

HE IS DEAD, MY LORD!

IS HE THE ONLY DEAD MAN? OR DO OTHERS ALSO DIE?

EVERYONE WHO IS BORN, HAS TO DIE SOME DAY.

I FEEL SICK, CHANNA. LET US RETURN TO THE PALACE.

*ON THE WAY BACK—*
STOP, CHANNA! WHO IS THAT? HE LOOKS CALM AND DIFFERENT FROM ALL THE OTHER MEN I HAVE SEEN.

HE IS A SAINT. HE HAS GIVEN UP A LIFE OF PLEASURE AND PAIN IN SEARCH OF TRUTH.

AT THE PALACE—

SIDDHARTHA! PLEASE TELL ME THE CAUSE OF YOUR UNHAPPINESS!

MOTHER, I HAVE LEARNT THAT ALL THINGS ALIVE AND BEAUTIFUL KEEP CHANGING. MEN GROW OLD. MEN FALL ILL AND DIE. I FEEL UNHAPPY WHEN I THINK OF THESE THINGS.

IN THE MIDDLE OF THE NIGHT, HE MADE THE DECISION.

I MUST FIND A WAY TO END SORROW. I WILL GO IN SEARCH OF TRUTH, LIKE THAT SAINT.

CHANNA GET MY HORSE READY! I WISH TO RIDE OUT.

YES, MASTER!

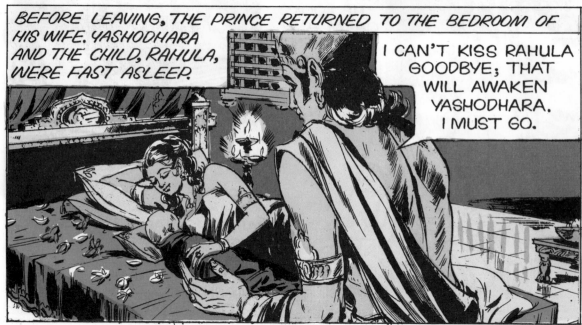

BEFORE LEAVING, THE PRINCE RETURNED TO THE BEDROOM OF HIS WIFE. YASHODHARA AND THE CHILD, RAHULA, WERE FAST ASLEEP.

I CAN'T KISS RAHULA GOODBYE; THAT WILL AWAKEN YASHODHARA. I MUST GO.

SIDDHARTHA MOUNTED HIS HORSE AND RODE OUT, ACCOMPANIED ONLY BY CHANNA.

ONCE THEY WERE OUTSIDE THE CITY, SIDDHARTHA GOT DOWN FROM THE HORSE.

CHANNA, TAKE ALL MY JEWELS AND RETURN TO KAPILAVASTU.

HE THEN CUT OFF HIS LONG HAIR AND WALKED ALONE.

LATER HE SAW A BEGGAR.

HALT, MY GOOD MAN! TAKE MY CLOTHES. AND GIVE ME YOURS.

WITH PLEASURE, MASTER.

SOON HE REACHED RAJAGRIHA, THE CAPITAL OF MAGADHA. HE WENT FROM HOUSE TO HOUSE SILENTLY WAITING TILL THE PEOPLE OFFERED HIM FOOD. KING BIMBISARA OBSERVED HIM FROM HIS PALACE.

LOOK AT THAT SAINT. HE LOOKS SO HANDSOME. FIND OUT WHO HE IS.

AS SOON AS THE MESSENGERS BROUGHT NEWS ABOUT SIDDHARTHA, KING BIMBISARA WENT TO MEET HIM.

YOU SEEM TO BELONG TO A NOBLE FAMILY. YOUR HAND SHOULD NOT HOLD A BEGGING BOWL, BUT THE REINS OF AN EMPIRE. I WILL GIVE YOU A HIGH POSITION IN MY KINGDOM. COME.

O KING, YOU ARE KIND. BUT I CANNOT ACCEPT YOUR INVITATION. I FEEL THAT LIFE IS FULL OF SORROW. I WISH TO FIND A WAY TO END ALL SORROW.

IF THAT IS YOUR WISH, I PRAY THAT YOU FIND IT. PLEASE COME AND TEACH ME WHEN YOU HAVE FOUND THE SOLUTION.

FROM RAJAGRIHA, SIDDHARTHA WENT IN SEARCH OF THE GREAT SAGES OF THOSE DAYS. NOT SATISFIED WITH THEIR TEACHINGS, HE ENTERED THE THICK JUNGLES OF URUBILVA, NEAR GAYA OF TODAY.

THERE WERE FIVE HERMITS IN THE JUNGLES OF URUBILVA.

THIS MAN IS KEEN ON HIS GOAL. HE IS SURE TO SUCCEED. LET US WAIT ON HIM.

SIDDHARTHA DRANK ONLY WATER AND ATE ONLY FRUITS AND HERBS. HE SLEPT ON THE HARD GROUND. AFTER SOME TIME HE STARTED EATING ONLY ONE HEMP GRAIN EVERY DAY. THIS MADE HIM VERY WEAK. ONE DAY, WHEN HE HAD GONE TO BATHE IN THE RIVER—

I FEEL WEAK. I DON'T HAVE STRENGTH TO GET UP.

HE CAUGHT HOLD OF A LOW BRANCH OF A TREE AND RAISED HIMSELF WITH ITS SUPPORT.

BUT AS HE BEGAN TO WALK AWAY FROM THE BANK, HE FELT WEAK AND FELL DOWN.

SLOWLY HE GOT UP.

NEXT DAY, AS HE SAT BENEATH A BANIAN TREE, SUJATA, DAUGHTER OF A HERDSMAN, CAME TO THAT SPOT. SHE OFFERED FOOD TO BUDDHA.

THANK YOU FOR FEEDING ME.

LATER—

HOW IS IT THAT YOU HAVE STARTED EATING FOOD AGAIN?

I HAVE COME TO BELIEVE THAT STARVING DOES NOT HELP IN REACHING THE TRUTH.

THE FIVE ASCETICS WERE DISAPPOINTED.

HE DOES NOT DESERVE OUR RESPECT.

YES, HE WANTS THE PLEASURES OF LIFE.

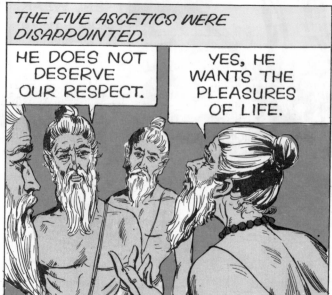

SIDDHARTHA NOW LIVED A LONELY LIFE.

THEY HAVE LEFT ME. LET THEM GO. BUT STARVING THE BODY IS NOT GOING TO HELP. I AM NOW SURE OF THAT.

HE MOVED TOWARDS A BODHI TREE AND SAT BENEATH IT.

HEAT AND COLD, HUNGER AND THIRST TROUBLED HIM. RAIN LASHED ON HIM.

COME WHAT MAY, I SHALL NOT MOVE FROM THIS SEAT TILL I FIND A WAY TO END SORROW.

VISIONS OF THE LIFE OF PLEASURE FLOATED BEFORE HIS EYES. BUT NOTHING COULD TEMPT HIM.

AND THEN HE SAW LIGHT.

SIDDHARTHA BECAME THE BUDDHA, THE ENLIGHTENED ONE.

I KNOW. I KNOW THE TRUTH NOW. THE WAY TO END SORROW IS FOUND.

HE SPENT SEVEN WEEKS UNDER THE TREE ENJOYING HIS STATE OF PERFECT HAPPINESS. THEN HE WENT OUT INTO THE WORLD TO TEACH OTHERS. FIRST, HE WENT TO BANARAS, IN SEARCH OF THE FIVE ASCETICS, WHO WERE WITH HIM IN URUBILVA. HE FOUND THEM IN DEER PARK.

HERE COMES SIDDHARTHA. HE RETURNED TO A LIFE OF EASE. LET US NOT TALK TO HIM.

BUT AS SOON AS HE CAME NEAR, THEY GOT UP AND RECEIVED HIM WITH RESPECT.

I HAVE COME TO TELL YOU WHAT I HAVE FOUND. LISTEN!

WHEN THEY HEARD THE BUDDHA, THEY BECAME HIS DISCIPLES. THE SANGHA THUS CAME INTO BEING.

THERE IS GREAT SORROW IN THIS WORLD. THIS SORROW IS BECAUSE OF DESIRE. IF YOU CAN FREE YOURSELF FROM DESIRE, YOU WILL BE FREE FROM SORROW. I WILL SHOW YOU THE WAY TO REMOVE SORROW FROM THE MIND.

AFTER THAT, HE RETURNED TO URUBILVA AND WENT TO THE HOUSE OF KASSHYAPA, A GREAT BRAHMAN.

WHAT DO YOU WANT?

I WANT TO SPEND A NIGHT HERE.

YOU ARE WELCOME. PLEASE COME IN.

KASSHYAPA WAS A WORSHIPPER OF AGNI, THE GOD OF FIRE.

MAY I STAY IN THE ROOM, WHERE YOU KEEP THE SACRED FIRE?

HAVEN'T YOU HEARD THAT THE SACRED FIRE IS GUARDED BY A SERPENT AT NIGHT? THE SERPENT WILL BITE YOU IF YOU GO NEAR THE FIRE.

I AM NOT AFRAID. PLEASE ALLOW ME TO SPEND THE NIGHT THERE.

AT LAST KASSHYAPA AGREED. BUDDHA SAT SILENTLY BEFORE THE FIRE. KASSHYAPA WENT TO SLEEP OUTSIDE.

EARLY NEXT MORNING –

LET ME GO AND LOOK FOR HIM. HE MUST BE DEAD. POOR MAN!

WHEN HE WENT INSIDE THE ROOM, HE SAW BUDDHA SITTING PEACEFULLY. THE LIGHT FROM THE FIRE SHONE ON HIS FACE.

I ACCEPT YOU AS MY MASTER. TEACH ME.

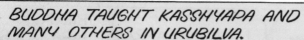

BUDDHA TAUGHT KASSHYAPA AND MANY OTHERS IN URUBILVA.

ONE DAY— MASTER, I HAVE HEARD THAT KING BIMBISARA WILL BE CELEBRATING A GREAT YAGNA.

LET US GO TO RAJAGRIHA.

ON THEIR WAY TO RAJAGRIHA, THEY SAW A HERD OF SHEEP. THERE WAS A LAME LAMB. BUDDHA LIFTED IT IN HIS ARMS.

POOR THING, IT MUST HAVE BEEN SUFFERING A LOT OF PAIN.

21

O KING, KILLING OF INNOCENT ANIMALS CANNOT BE A GOOD DEED. THE WAY TO HAPPINESS DOES NOT LIE IN YAGNA.

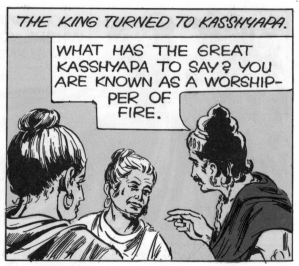

THE KING TURNED TO KASSHYAPA.

WHAT HAS THE GREAT KASSHYAPA TO SAY? YOU ARE KNOWN AS A WORSHIPPER OF FIRE.

KASSHYAPA BOWED TO BUDDHA.

I AM A DISCIPLE OF BUDDHA.

I SEE. BUDDHA IS THE TEACHER. DON'T YOU ALSO BELIEVE IN YAGNA?

BUDDHA HAS SHOWN ME THE RIGHT WAY NEITHER THE WORSHIP OF FIRE NOR THE SACRIFICE OF DUMB ANIMALS CAN MAKE US FREE FROM SORROW.

THE KING TURNED TO BUDDHA.

MASTER, LET US HEAR YOUR WORDS OF WISDOM.

AND BUDDHA TAUGHT THEM.

LORD, I HAVE GIVEN UP THE IDEA OF PERFORMING YAGNA. I TAKE REFUGE IN BUDDHA.

NEXT DAY, THE KING INVITED BUDDHA AND HIS DISCIPLES FOR A MEAL AT HIS PALACE. AFTER THE MEAL WAS OVER—

LORD, I GIVE VENUVANA, MY GARDEN AS A GIFT TO THE SANGHA. PLEASE ACCEPT IT.

ONE DAY, KRISHA GOTAMI BROUGHT BEFORE BUDDHA HER DEAD CHILD.

MASTER, PLEASE BRING IT BACK TO LIFE. IT IS MY ONLY CHILD.

CONTROL YOUR GRIEF. DO AS I SAY. GET ME A FEW MUSTARD SEEDS FROM ANY HOUSE, WHERE NO DEATH HAS TAKEN PLACE. AND I WILL BRING BACK TO LIFE YOUR CHILD.

FROM HOUSE TO HOUSE KRISHA GOTAMI WENT.

I LOST MY HUSBAND LAST YEAR!

I LOST MY TWO CHILDREN.

MY MOTHER DIED YESTERDAY.

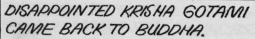

LORD! I COULD NOT FIND A PLACE WHERE NO DEATH HAS OCCURRED.

MY CHILD ALL THAT IS BORN, MUST DIE ONE DAY. THERE IS ULTIMATELY NOTHING BUT SORROW IN LIFE. IT IS FREEDOM FROM DESIRE THAT FREES US FROM SORROW.

AFTER A FEW YEARS, AT SUDDHODANA'S COURT_

LORD! OUR PRINCE HAS BECOME FAMOUS. MANY HAVE BECOME HIS DISCIPLES. THEY ARE SPREADING HIS TEACHINGS.

GO TO SIDDHARTHA AND TELL HIM THAT I AM GROWING OLD AND WISH TO SEE HIM BEFORE I DIE.

WHEN BUDDHA REACHED KAPILAVASTU_

WELCOME MY SON! I WISH YOU WOULD BECOME KING.

I AM SORRY. I HAVE CHOSEN THE PATH OF PEACE.

THE KING ARRANGED FOR BUDDHA'S STAY IN A GROVE NEARBY.

WHERE IS YASHODHARA?

SHE HAS REFUSED TO COME.

SHE HAS BEEN VERY UN-HAPPY EVER SINCE YOU LEFT. SHE HAS CUT HER HAIR, WEARS SIMPLE CLOTHES AND EATS SPARINGLY JUST AS YOU DID.

WITH TWO OF HIS DISCIPLES, BUDDHA WENT TO YASHODHARA'S CHAMBER.

I MUST TRY TO HEAL THE SORROW IN HER HEART.

WHEN YASHODHARA SAW BUDDHA, SHE FELL AT HIS FEET AND WEPT.

THEN REMEMBERING THAT OTHERS WERE PRESENT, SHE GOT UP AND SAT AT A LITTLE DISTANCE.

BUDDHA SPOKE WORDS OF COMFORT.

A WEEK AFTER · BUDDHA CAME TO KAPILAVASTU.

RAHULA, DO YOU SEE THE MAN SITTING THERE IN THE CENTRE? HE IS YOUR FATHER. GO TO HIM AND ASK FOR YOUR SHARE OF HIS PROPERTY.

RAHULA WENT TO BUDDHA.

FATHER! MY MOTHER SENT ME TO ASK YOU FOR MY SHARE OF YOUR PROPERTY.

BUDDHA TURNED TO SARI-PUTRA, HIS DISCIPLE.

MY SON ASKS FOR HIS INHERITANCE. WELL THEN, TAKE HIM IN THE SANGHA.

AFTER RAHULA JOINED THE SANGHA, MANY YOUNG MEN OF THE ROYAL FAMILY ALSO JOINED. AMONGST THEM WAS DEVADATTA. HE ALSO MOVED ABOUT WITH BUDDHA. ONE DAY—

MASTER, YOU SHOULD REST. I SHALL LEAD THE SANGHA.

NO, DEVA-DATTA THE SANGHA STILL NEEDS MY GUIDANCE.

DEVADATTA FELT JEALOUS OF BUDDHA. HE WENT TO RAJAGRIHA AND MET AJATASATRU, SON OF KING BIMBISARA.

PRINCE AJATASATRU! HOW LONG CAN YOU WAIT TO BECOME A KING? PUT YOUR FATHER IN PRISON AND BE A KING YOURSELF.

IT IS A GOOD IDEA, DEVADATTA. I WILL DO AS YOU SAY.

AJATASATRU DID AS DEVA-DATTA ADVISED HIM.

IT IS NICE TO BE A KING. THANK YOU, DEVADATTA! IF YOU WANT MY HELP IN ANYTHING, ASK FOR IT.

I NEED YOUR HELP, KING AJATASATRU. HELP ME KILL BUDDHA. I HATE HIM.

DEVADATTA TRIED MANY WAYS TO KILL BUDDHA.

LOOK OUT! A BIG STONE IS ROLLING DOWN TOWARDS BUDDHA.

SIT WHERE YOU ARE. NO HARM WILL COME TO ME.

THE ROCK SPLIT INTO TWO AND A PIECE FELL ON EITHER SIDE OF BUDDHA.

MANY OF DEVADATTA'S FOLLOWERS CAME TO JOIN THE SANGHA OF BUDDHA.

THE ROCK DID NOT KILL HIM.

HE LOOKS FRAIL, BUT HE IS GREAT. LET US GO TO HIM.

I HEAR, MANY OF MY FOLLOWERS HAVE JOINED HIS SANGHA. WHY NOT SET AN ELEPHANT ON HIM?

YET ANOTHER ORDER FROM AJATA-SATRU.

INTOXICATE THE ELEPHANT NALAGIRI, AND THEN LET HIM LOOSE IN THE PATH OF BUDDHA.

RUN, RUN, NALAGIRI IS FREE. HE HAS RUINED HALF THE TOWN ALREADY. TWENTY MEN HAVE BEEN KILLED.

MASTER, LET US HIDE. A WILD ELEPHANT IS COMING THIS WAY.

NO, HE WON'T HARM US.

NALAGIRI CAME THUMPING ALONG AND RUSHED TOWARDS BUDDHA IN A MAD FURY.

BUDDHA SMILED AND RAISED HIS HAND. THE ELEPHANT, AT ONCE CALMED, KNELT AT HIS FEET.

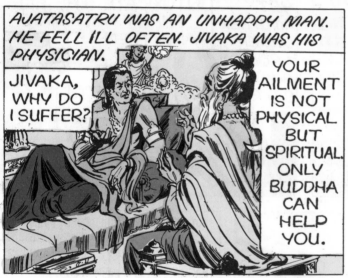

AJATASATRU WAS AN UNHAPPY MAN. HE FELL ILL OFTEN. JIVAKA WAS HIS PHYSICIAN.

JIVAKA, WHY DO I SUFFER?

YOUR AILMENT IS NOT PHYSICAL BUT SPIRITUAL. ONLY BUDDHA CAN HELP YOU.

LET US GO TO HIM, THEN. WHERE WILL HE BE NOW?

IN THE AMRAVANA, AT VAISHALI..

.WHICH BELONGS TO AMRAPALI, THE COURTESAN?

YES, MY LORD! AMRAPALI HAS GIFTED IT TO BUDDHA.

WHEN AJATASATRU REACHED AMRAVANA—

I HEARD NO SOUND. WHERE IS BUDDHA?

HE IS HERE WITH OVER TWELVE HUNDRED DISCIPLES

AJATASATRU'S MIND TROUBLED HIM.

TWELVE HUNDRED PEOPLE! NOT A SOUND OF HUMAN HABITATION HERE!! HAVE YOU BROUGHT ME HERE TO BE KILLED? IS IT A PLOT OF YOURS?

MY LORD! TRUST ME. LET US GO AHEAD.

AND AJATASATRU WAS SPELL-BOUND WHEN HE SAW THE ASSEMBLY OF MEN LISTENING QUIETLY TO THE GREAT TEACHER.

ALL SUFFERING AND PAIN, FEAR AND HATRED, COME FROM DESIRE. THE MAN WHO IS FREE FROM ALL DESIRE, NEED NOT WORRY. WHOM HAS HE TO FEAR?

HOW SOOTHING!

AJATASATRU BECAME A DISCIPLE OF BUDDHA.

NOT MUCH LATER, DEVADATTA ALSO REPENTED. ONE DAY, HE SAID TO HIS FOLLOWERS—

CHILDREN, TAKE ME TO BUDDHA. HE ALONE CAN BRING PEACE TO MY TROUBLED MIND.

THE MEN CARRYING DEVADATTA KEPT DOWN THE LITTER AND WENT TO REFRESH THEMSELVES.

WHERE HAVE MY MEN GONE? I AM IN A HURRY TO MEET BUDDHA.

BEFORE HE COULD REACH BUDDHA, HE TOTTERED AND FELL.

I AM DYING. BUT NOW I KNOW THAT BUDDHA IS INDEED THE ENLIGHTENED ONE – THE TEACHER OF ALL. I TAKE REFUGE IN HIM.

BUDDHAM SARANAM GACCHAMI

DHAMMAM SARANAM GACCHAMI

SANGHAM SARANAM GACCHAMI

BUDDHA LIVED TO A RIPE OLD AGE. MILLIONS TOOK REFUGE IN HIM AND IN HIS TEACHINGS. PEOPLE, WHO SPOKE DIFFERENT LANGUAGES AND BELONGED TO DISTANT LANDS BECAME HIS FOLLOWERS.

# KING KUSHA

## A JATAKA STORY ABOUT INNER BEAUTY

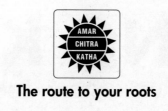

**The route to your roots**

# KING KUSHA

Kusha, prince of Kushavati was blessed with immense wisdom and extraordinary talent but he had the ugliest of faces. The beautiful princess Prabhavati was not aware of his ugliness when she married him. Kusha's mother saw to it that the princess never set eyes on her son's face. But when she did, Prabhavati refused to have anything to do with her husband and went away leaving poor Kusha broken-hearted.

| Script | Illustrations | Editor |
|---|---|---|
| Kamala Chandrakant | Souren Roy | Anant Pai |

*Cover illustration by: Pratap Mulick*

# KING KUSHA

SHEELAVATI, THE CHIEF QUEEN OF THE HEIRLESS KING OKKAKA OF KUSHAVATI, WAS OFFERED A BOON BY INDRA, KING OF THE GODS.

YOU SHALL HAVE TWO SONS. ONE WISE BUT UGLY, THE OTHER HANDSOME BUT A FOOL. WHICH WILL YOU HAVE FIRST?

THE WISE ONE, MY LORD.

IN DUE COURSE, SHEELAVATI GAVE BIRTH TO A SON.

HE SHALL BE CALLED KUSHA.

TWO YEARS LATER, SHE GAVE BIRTH TO THE SECOND SON—JAYAMPATI.

WHAT A BEAUTIFUL BABY!

EVEN AS A CHILD, KUSHA WAS CONSCIOUS OF HIS APPEARANCE.

I MUST EXCEL IN ALL THE ARTS TO MAKE UP FOR MY UGLY LOOKS.

IN THE YEARS THAT FOLLOWED, KUSHA MASTERED THE ARTS OF MUSIC, PAINTING AND SCULPTURE. ONE DAY—

SHEELAVATI, KUSHA IS ALMOST SIXTEEN YEARS OLD. I WOULD LIKE TO PLACE HIM ON THE THRONE WHILE I AM YET ALIVE. BUT BEFORE I DO, I'D LIKE TO SEE HIM MARRIED.

I TOO WOULD LOVE TO HAVE A DAUGHTER IN THE PALACE!

WHEN KUSHA LEARNT OF HIS PARENTS' WISHES HE WAS SAD.

WOULD ANY PRINCESS MARRY AN UGLY FELLOW LIKE ME?

BUT I CANNOT TELL MY PARENTS THIS. IT WOULD HURT THEM. I MUST FIND A WAY OUT.

AFTER GIVING THE MATTER A GREAT DEAL OF THOUGHT, HE HIT UPON A PLAN.

I WILL CREATE A BEAUTIFUL IMAGE AND ASK FOR THE IMPOSSIBLE—SOMEONE EXACTLY LIKE IT FOR A WIFE.

WHEN THE IMAGE WAS COMPLETED, KUSHA COULD NOT HELP ADMIRING HIS OWN WORK.

THEY WILL NEVER BE ABLE TO FIND A PRINCESS HALF AS BEAUTIFUL AS YOU!

HE THEN BROUGHT HIS MOTHER TO SEE IT.

IF YOU CAN FIND ME A PRINCESS AS BEAUTIFUL AS THIS, I'LL MARRY HER.

PRINCE KUSHA, THE GIFT OF INDRA, IS HIGHLY TALENTED. HE WILL HAVE NONE BUT A PRINCESS WORTHY OF HIM.

TAKE THIS FIGURE HE HAS CREATED AND TOUR THE COUNTRY EXHIBITING IT. WHEN YOU COME ACROSS ITS LIVING LIKENESS, PRESENT THE IMAGE TO HER FATHER AND REQUEST HIM FOR HER HAND ON BEHALF OF YOUR KING.

THE COUNCILLORS TRAVELLED FROM KINGDOM TO KINGDOM, EXHIBITING THE IMAGE, TILL AT LAST THEY ARRIVED AT SAGALA, THE CAPITAL OF THE KINGDOM OF MADDA.

AS USUAL, THEY PLACED THE IMAGE AT A CONSPICUOUS SPOT. THEN—

NOW LET US STAND AWAY FROM IT AND OVERHEAR THE COMMENTS OF THOSE WHO PASS BY.

AFTER A WHILE, A HUNCHBACK FOLLOWED BY SEVEN OR EIGHT MAIDS CAME BY.

AS SOON AS WE'VE BATHED WE WILL···

PRABHAVATI! WHAT ON EARTH ARE YOU DOING ALONE HERE AT THIS HOUR? SHOULD YOUR FATHER HEAR OF THIS IT WILL BE THE END OF US.

OO-OO-OO! MY HAND!

IT'S A METAL IMAGE!

MADAM! WHAT'S THE MATTER? YOUR HAND! IT'S BRUISED AND BROKEN!

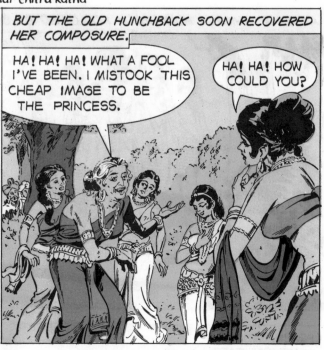

BUT THE OLD HUNCHBACK SOON RECOVERED HER COMPOSURE.

HA! HA! HA! WHAT A FOOL I'VE BEEN. I MISTOOK THIS CHEAP IMAGE TO BE THE PRINCESS.

HA! HA! HOW COULD YOU?

I HAVE HURT MY HANDS FOR INSULTING HER. WHAT IS THIS WORTHLESS IMAGE COMPARED TO MY DARLING PRABHAVATI!

THE COUNCILLORS WERE OVERJOYED.

WHAT DO YOU MEAN?

WHAT I SAY. THIS IMAGE WOULD APPEAR UGLY BEFORE HER. AND I AM HER NURSE WHO SAYS SO.

THE DELIGHTED COUNCILLORS IMMEDIATELY SOUGHT AN AUDIENCE WITH PRABHAVATI'S FATHER.

YOUR MAJESTY, OUR KING, OKKAKA OF KUSHAVATI, IS ANXIOUS TO PLACE HIS SON, THE BRAVE PRINCE KUSHA, ON THE THRONE. WE REQUEST YOU ON HIS BEHALF FOR THE HAND OF PRINCESS PRABHAVATI.

WE GLADLY AGREE. WE WOULD BE HONOURED BY THE ALLIANCE.

BACK AT KUSHAVATI—

YOUR MAJESTY, WE HAVE FOUND HER—A PRINCESS MORE BEAUTIFUL THAN THE IMAGE!

WHEN KING OKKAKA AND QUEEN SHEELAVATI HEARD THE WHOLE STORY—

LET US SET OUT FOR SAGALA AT ONCE WITH A LARGE RETINUE.

YES! LET US NOT WASTE A MOMENT.

WHEN THEY REACHED SAGALA, THEY WERE RECEIVED GRACIOUSLY BY THE KING, THE QUEEN, PRINCESS PRABHAVATI AND HER SEVEN YOUNGER SISTERS.

LATER, WHEN PRABHAVATI CAME TO PAY HER RESPECTS TO SHEELAVATI —

SHOULD THIS DAZZLING BEAUTY SEE MY SON'S FACE, SHE WILL RUN AWAY FROM HIM THAT VERY MOMENT. YET I MUST NOT FAIL MY SON. LET ME SEE WHAT I CAN DO.

WHEN PRABHAVATI HAD LEFT, SHEELAVATI SPOKE TO THE KING OF MADDA.

YOUR DAUGHTER IS WORTHY OF MY SON. BUT...

YES?

WE HAVE AN UNUSUAL TRADITION. IF SHE WILL AGREE TO OBSERVE IT WE WILL TAKE HER AS OUR DAUGHTER-IN-LAW.

WHAT IS THE TRADITION?

A WIFE IS NOT PERMITTED TO SEE HER HUSBAND'S FACE TILL SHE HAS CONCEIVED. WILL SHE AGREE?

PRABHAVATI AGREED TO RESPECT THE TRADITION AND AFTER MUCH GIVING AND RECEIVING OF GIFTS, OKKAKA AND SHEELAVATI ESCORTED THEIR DAUGHTER-IN-LAW, ALONG WITH HER NURSE AND A VAST RETINUE, TO KUSHAVATI.

BACK AT KUSHAVATI —

HAVE THE CITY DECORATED. RELEASE ALL PRISONERS. THE WEDDING AND THE CORONATION OF PRINCE KUSHA SHALL BE CELEBRATED TODAY!

NEITHER KUSHA NOR PRABHAVATI SAW EACH OTHER'S FACE. BUT—

HOW WELL HE PLAYS THE VEENA!* HE MUST HAVE THE SENSITIVE FACE OF A MUSICIAN.

AH! I CAN ONLY IMAGINE HOW SHE LOOKS BY THINKING OF MY GOLDEN IMAGE.

A FEW DAYS AFTER THE WEDDING, KING KUSHA CAME TO SHEELAVATI.

MOTHER, PLEASE PERMIT ME TO LOOK AT MY WIFE BUT ONCE.

YOU WILL HAVE TO WAIT UNTIL SHE HAS CONCEIVED.

* LUTE-LIKE INSTRUMENT

I CANNOT WAIT TILL THEN, MOTHER.

ALL RIGHT. GO TO THE ELEPHANT STALLS DISGUISED AS A KEEPER. I WILL BRING PRABHAVATI THERE. BUT SEE THAT YOU DO NOT MAKE YOURSELF KNOWN TO HER.

SHEELAVATI THEN WENT TO PRABHAVATI.

YOU HAVE NOT YET SEEN YOUR LORD'S ELEPHANTS. COME, I WILL SHOW THEM TO YOU.

WHEN KUSHA SAW PRABHAVATI AS SHE WALKED BEHIND HIS MOTHER, HE WAS ENCHANTED.

IS SHE A PRINCESS OR A GODDESS?

DETERMINED TO FIND OUT, HE PICKED UP A HANDFUL OF DUNG AND FLUNG IT AT HER.

11

PRABHAVATI WAS ENRAGED.

HOW DARE YOU! YOU UGLY FELLOW. I WILL GET THE KING, MY HUSBAND, TO CUT OFF YOUR HANDS.

SHE IS A PRINCESS!

AS SHEELAVATI PACIFIED HER AND HURRIED HER AWAY—

MOTHER, I MUST SEE MY HUSBAND'S FACE—JUST ONCE.

NO! PLEASE DON'T ASK FOR THAT. IT WOULD BE INAUSPICIOUS.

BUT PRABHAVATI WENT ON PLEADING. AT LAST—

WELL, TOMORROW MY SON WILL BE RIDING THROUGH THE CITY. YOU CAN OPEN YOUR WINDOW AND SEE HIM.

I WILL TELL KUSHA TO SEND JAYAMPATI IN A PROCESSION THROUGH THE STREETS. HE CAN WEAR KUSHA'S CLOTHES AND RIDE ON HIS ELEPHANT.

POOR KUSHA WAS NOT GOING TO MISS THE CHANCE OF SEEING HIS WIFE AGAIN.

DRESSED AS AN ELEPHANT-KEEPER, I WILL RIDE BEHIND JAYAMPATI.

THE NEXT DAY WHEN PRABHAVATI SAW JAYAMPATI —

HOW HANDSOME MY HUSBAND IS! INDEED! I AM PROUD OF HIM.

BUT WHAT AN IMPUDENT ELEPHANT-KEEPER HE HAS! HOW DARE HE WAVE TO ME!

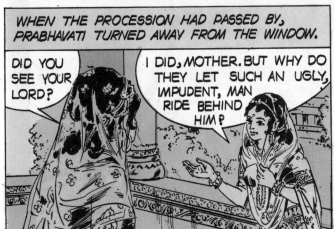

WHEN THE PROCESSION HAD PASSED BY, PRABHAVATI TURNED AWAY FROM THE WINDOW.

DID YOU SEE YOUR LORD?

I DID, MOTHER. BUT WHY DO THEY LET SUCH AN UGLY, IMPUDENT, MAN RIDE BEHIND HIM?

DON'T BE MISLED BY LOOKS. THAT MAN IS CAPABLE AND THE KING MUST HAVE A CAPABLE MAN SITTING BEHIND HIM.

BUT PRABHAVATI WAS NOT CONVINCED.

NO MAN WOULD BE ALLOWED TO BEHAVE LIKE THAT HOWEVER EXCELLENT HIS SERVICES MIGHT BE. CAN IT BE THAT HE IS KING KUSHA AND THEY DO NOT LET ME SEE HIM BECAUSE HE IS SO UGLY?

SHE TURNED TO HER NURSE.

RUN, MY DEAR. FIND OUT WHO WAS THE KING— THE MAN IN FRONT OR THE ONE BEHIND.

HOW AM I TO FIND OUT?

THE KING WILL BE THE FIRST TO ALIGHT FROM THE ELEPHANT. GO. DON'T WASTE ANY MORE TIME.

WHEN THE NURSE SAW KUSHA ALIGHT FIRST, SHE WAS SHOCKED.

WHAT! IS THAT HIDEOUS ONE KING KUSHA!

AH! ISN'T THAT PRABHAVATI'S NURSE? SHE IS HERE TO SPY ON ME.

HE SENT FOR HER.

I CHARGE YOU ON PAIN OF DEATH NOT TO REVEAL MY SECRET.

SHE WENT BACK TO PRABHAVATI WHO EAGERLY AWAITED HER RETURN.

THE ONE THAT SAT IN FRONT WAS THE FIRST TO ALIGHT.

THANK GOD!

THE SECOND SIGHT OF PRABHAVATI MADE KUSHA WANT TO SEE HER YET AGAIN. HE SPOKE TO HIS MOTHER.

WELL THEN, IF YOU MUST, ENTER THE LOTUS POOL, CONCEAL YOURSELF AND WAIT.

A LITTLE LATER, SHEELAVATI BROUGHT PRABHAVATI TO THE GARDEN.

OH! WHAT A BEAUTIFUL LOTUS POND. MOTHER, MAY I BATHE IN IT?

CERTAINLY. I'LL GO BACK TO THE PALACE, AND SEND SOME MAIDS WITH A CHANGE OF CLOTHES FOR YOU.

AH! THAT LOTUS IS LARGER AND MORE BEAUTIFUL THAN THE REST. I'LL PLUCK IT FOR MYSELF.

AS SHE STRETCHED OUT HER HAND TO PLUCK IT—

EE-EE-AH! A GOBLIN HAS CAUGHT HOLD OF ME.

I AM KING KUSHA!

PRABHAVATI SWOONED.

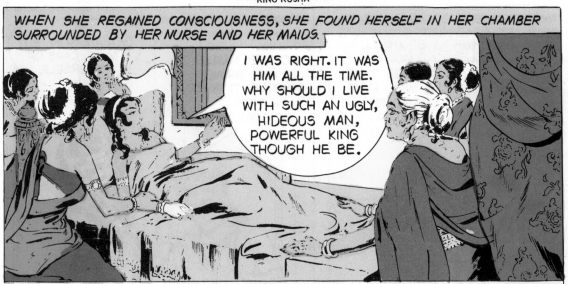

WHEN SHE REGAINED CONSCIOUSNESS, SHE FOUND HERSELF IN HER CHAMBER SURROUNDED BY HER NURSE AND HER MAIDS.

I WAS RIGHT. IT WAS HIM ALL THE TIME. WHY SHOULD I LIVE WITH SUCH AN UGLY, HIDEOUS MAN, POWERFUL KING THOUGH HE BE.

SHE SUMMONED THE COUNCILLORS WHO HAD SPOKEN TO HER FATHER.

HAVE MY CHARIOT READY. I WILL RETURN THIS VERY DAY TO MY PARENTS.

B—BUT... YES, YOUR MAJESTY.

NOT KNOWING WHAT TO DO, THEY WENT AND CONSULTED KUSHA.

DO NOT STOP HER. SHE WOULD BE UN-HAPPY. I WILL GO AFTER HER LATER AND BRING HER BACK WITH HER CONSENT.

THOUGH KUSHA SO KIND-HEART-EDLY LET PRABHAVATI GO, HE WAS DESOLATE. TWO DAYS LATER —

BY THIS TIME SHE WILL HAVE REACHED SAGALA.

HE WENT TO HIS MOTHER.

MOTHER, I WILL GO AND BRING PRABHAVATI BACK, WITH HER CONSENT.

GO, MY SON. BUT TAKE CARE OF YOURSELF.

EQUIPPING HIMSELF WITH ALL THAT HE WOULD NEED, KUSHA SET OUT FOR SAGALA.

I WILL NOT REST TILL I WIN HER LOVE.

WHEN HE REACHED SAGALA, HE ENTERED THE PALACE AND FOUND HIS WAY TO THE ELEPHANT STALLS.

WHO ARE YOU? WHAT DO YOU WANT?

LET ME STAY HERE FOR THE NIGHT AND I WILL PLAY THE VEENA FOR YOU.

THEY AGREED. KUSHA TUNED HIS VEENA AND BEGAN TO PLAY.

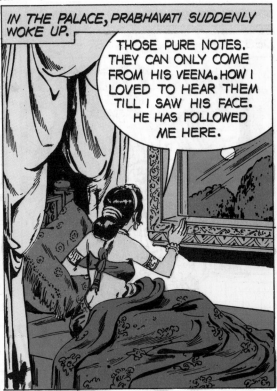

IN THE PALACE, PRABHAVATI SUDDENLY WOKE UP.

THOSE PURE NOTES. THEY CAN ONLY COME FROM HIS VEENA. HOW I LOVED TO HEAR THEM TILL I SAW HIS FACE. HE HAS FOLLOWED ME HERE.

EARLY NEXT MORNING, KUSHA WOKE UP.

I MUST NOW TRY TO MEET PRABHAVATI WITHOUT LETTING ANYONE KNOW WHO I AM.

HE WENT TO THE ROYAL POTTER AND BECAME HIS APPRENTICE. A FEW DAYS LATER—

WHY, MY SON, YOU ARE TALENTED! THESE VASES ARE BEAUTIFUL! I SHALL TAKE THEM TO THE PALACE RIGHT AWAY.

MASTER, DO NOT FORGET. THIS ONE WITH THESE FIGURES IS FOR PRINCESS PRABHAVATI. I MADE IT SPECIALLY FOR HER.

AT THE PALACE —

WHO HAS MADE THESE EXQUISITE? VASES?

I HAVE, YOUR MAJESTY.

THIS IS NOT YOUR HANDI-WORK. TELL ME THE TRUTH. WHO MADE THEM?

M-MY APPRENTICE, YOUR MAJESTY.

NOT YOUR APPRENTICE BUT YOUR MASTER. HENCEFORTH HE SHALL MAKE ALL THE POTTERY FOR MY DAUGHTERS. YOU MAY TAKE THE VASES TO THEM, HOWEVER. AH! YOU MAY GIVE HIM THESE GOLD COINS.

WHEN THE PRINCESSES SAW THE VASES —

HOW DELIGHTFUL THEY ARE!

LOOK AT THIS ONE. I'LL KEEP IT.

SUCH EXQUISITE WORKMANSHIP!

KUSHA LEFT THE POTTER AND APPRENTICED HIMSELF TO THE ROYAL WICKER-WORKER. A FEW DAYS LATER—

WHOEVER HE IS, HE IS THE BEST WORKER I'VE HAD SO FAR. HOW DEFTLY HIS FINGERS MOVE.

WHAT ARE YOU MAKING?

A PALM LEAF FAN FOR THE ELDEST PRINCESS. SEE, HERE SHE IS, STANDING BY THIS PILLAR.

REMARKABLE WORKMANSHIP! I SHALL TAKE IT TO THE KING RIGHT AWAY.

AT THE PALACE—

WHOSE WORK IS THIS? NOT YOURS, I'M CERTAIN.

IT'S THE CREATION OF MY NEW APPRENTICE, SIR.

NOT YOUR APPRENTICE BUT YOUR MASTER. GIVE HIM THESE GOLD COINS.

THE MOMENT PRABHAVATI SAW THE FAN, HOWEVER—

THIS, TOO, IS HIS HANDI-WORK. WHY DOES HE PURSUE ME?

SHE FLUNG THE FAN ON THE FLOOR.

DON'T YOU DARE SHOW ME SUCH INFERIOR WORK EVER AGAIN.

HA! HA! IT WAS NOT KING KUSHA WHO MADE THAT FAN. SO WHY DO YOU DISOWN IT, PRABHAVATI?

THE WICKER-WORKER RETURNED, AND TOLD KUSHA ALL THAT HAPPENED AT THE PALACE.

···WOMEN ARE STRANGE. I DON'T KNOW WHY SHE THREW IT ON THE FLOOR IN A RAGE.

KUSHA KNEW.

I WILL HAVE TO TRY SOME OTHER MEANS TO MEET HER.

HE PONDERED FOR A WHILE. THEN—

I KNOW WHAT. I SHALL SEEK SERVICE IN THE ROYAL KITCHEN. PERHAPS...

KUSHA WAS LUCKY. THE ROYAL COOK HAD SACKED ONE OF HIS ASSISTANTS THAT VERY DAY.

AND DON'T EVER LET ME SEE YOU NEAR THE ROYAL KITCHEN AGAIN.

SO THE MOMENT KUSHA APPROACHED THE ROYAL COOK —

IN FACT, I NEED A HELP. BUT YOU WILL HAVE TO COOK YOUR OWN MEAL IN THE KITCHEN MEANT FOR MENIALS.

THAT IS NO PROBLEM, SIR.

KUSHA SOON BECAME AN EXPERT COOK— BETTER EVEN THAN HIS MASTER. ONE DAY—

HERE, YOU MAY COOK THIS CHOP FOR YOURSELF.

AN HOUR LATER, AS THE KING WAS BEING SERVED —

MM—M—M! WHAT A DELICIOUS AROMA. IS THAT DISH YET TO COME?

N-NO, YOUR MAJESTY. WHAT YOU SMELL IS THE CHOP MY NEW ASSISTANT IS COOKING FOR HIMSELF.

THEN LET ME TASTE IT.

AFTER THE KING HAD TASTED IT —

HENCEFORTH YOUR ASSISTANT SHALL COOK FOR ME AND MY DAUGHTERS AH! AND GIVE HIM THESE GOLD COINS.

KUSHA WAS EXTREMELY HAPPY WHEN HE HEARD ABOUT THE KING'S ORDER.

PLEASE KEEP THE COINS FOR YOURSELF, MASTER. I HAVE NO USE FOR THEM.

AT LAST I SHALL BE ABLE TO SEE MY WIFE.

THE NEXT DAY—

I FEEL SORRY FOR HIM. YET I MUST NOT LET HIM KNOW THAT I DO OR HE WILL STAY ON, THINKING I'VE YIELDED.

KUSHA, I CAN'T BEAR THE SIGHT OF YOUR UGLY FACE. GO BACK TO KUSHAVATI. IT IS NOT RIGHT FOR YOU TO WASTE YOUR TIME HERE.

I AM NOT GOING BACK WITHOUT YOU. I WANT YOUR LOVE AND NOT THE THRONE. I WOULD GLADLY GIVE UP CROWN AND THRONE TO LIVE NEAR YOU.

WHEN PRABHAVATI HEARD THIS SHE WAS ALARMED.

SUPPOSE HE DECLARES "I AM KING KUSHA" AND SEIZES MY HAND. NO ONE WILL STOP HIM. BESIDES, SOMEONE MIGHT OVERHEAR OUR TALK.

TO DISCOURAGE ANY FURTHER DIALOGUE, SHE CLOSED THE DOOR AND BOLTED IT.

KUSHA GAZED FOR A MOMENT AT THE CLOSED DOOR, AND THEN WENT DOWN.

SHE IS BOUND TO RELENT. I WILL WAIT PATIENTLY.

BUT SEVEN LONG MONTHS PASSED AND KUSHA TOILED ON. AT LAST—

IN SEVEN MONTHS, SHE HAS NOT SO MUCH AS LET ME HAVE A GLIMPSE OF HER. WHY DO I PINE FOR HER? SHE IS HARSH AND CRUEL. I WILL RETURN TO MY KING-DOM AND MY PARENTS.

AT THAT MOMENT, REALISING HOW DISAPPOINTED KUSHA WAS, INDRA DECIDED TO HELP HIM.

I WILL SEND THE SAME MESSAGE TO SEVEN DIFFERENT KINGS, SAYING "PRABHAVATI HAS LEFT KING KUSHA AND RETURNED HOME. I OFFER HER HAND TO YOU."

TELL EACH KING THAT YOU COME FROM THE COURT OF MADDA.

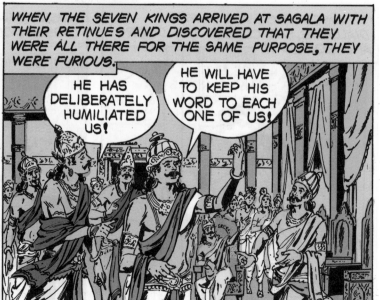

WHEN THE SEVEN KINGS ARRIVED AT SAGALA WITH THEIR RETINUES AND DISCOVERED THAT THEY WERE ALL THERE FOR THE SAME PURPOSE, THEY WERE FURIOUS.

HE HAS DELIBERATELY HUMILIATED US!

HE WILL HAVE TO KEEP HIS WORD TO EACH ONE OF US!

THEY SENT A MESSAGE TO THE KING.

GIVE PRABHAVATI TO ALL SEVEN OF US OR PREPARE FOR WAR.

THE KING WAS ALARMED.

I WILL HAVE TO CUT HER UP INTO SEVEN PIECES AND SEND ONE TO EACH MONARCH.

HOW CAN YOU DO SUCH A CRUEL THING TO YOUR OWN DAUGHTER?

IF I SEND HER TO ANY ONE OF THEM IT WILL BE WAR WITH THE OTHER SIX.

WHY DID SHE REJECT A HUSBAND AS POWERFUL AS KING KUSHA? LET HER SUFFER FOR IT.

WHEN PRABHAVATI HEARD OF HER FATHER'S DECISION, SHE WAS TERRIFIED.

SHE RAN TO HER MOTHER'S CHAMBER.

MOTHER!

O PRABHAVATI, I AM HELPLESS. IF ONLY KING KUSHA WERE HERE.

HE IS HERE, MOTHER. COME I'LL TAKE YOU TO HIM.

PRABHAVATI LED HER MOTHER TO THE KITCHEN.

LOOK! THERE HE IS— IN THE GUISE OF A COOK. HE CAME HERE FOR MY SAKE.

SHE RAN FORWARD AND FELL AT KUSHA'S FEET.

MY LORD, FORGIVE ME. I HAVE DONE YOU GREAT WRONG. I AM TO PAY FOR IT WITH MY LIFE. YES. THIS BEAUTIFUL BODY OF MINE, OF WHICH I WAS SO VAIN IS TO BE CUT INTO PIECES, TO BE GIVEN TO SEVEN KINGS, TO PREVENT A WAR.

WHAT! WILL ANYONE DARE TOUCH MY DEAR WIFE WHEN I AM YET ALIVE!

B—BUT! WH—WHAT ABOUT THE SEVEN KINGS?

LEAVE THAT TO ME. GO. BATHE AND ADORN YOURSELF AND WAIT FOR ME IN YOUR PALACE.

KUSHA SETTLED MATTERS BY OFFERING HIS SEVEN SISTERS-IN-LAW TO THE SEVEN KINGS.

THEN HE AND PRABHAVATI WENT TO KUSHAVATI WHERE THEY LIVED HAPPILY EVER AFTER.

31

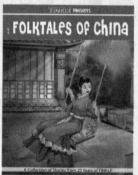

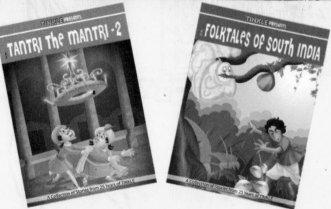

# ANGULIMALA

## THE BANDIT WHO TOOK REFUGE IN BUDDHA

www.amarchitrakatha.com

**The route to your roots**

# ANGULIMALA

The bandit wore a gruesome garland of fingers of the men he had killed. As his garland of fingers grew longer strong men cowered in fright. The bandit was invincible – until he met a gentle monk – Buddha. Thus darkness came face to face with light and at last the restless bandit found peace.

**Script**
Subba Rao

**Illustrations**
Pratap Mulick

**Editor**
Anant Pai

# ANGULIMALA

LONG, LONG AGO, A KING CALLED PRASENAJIT RULED OVER KOSALA* FROM HIS CAPITAL, SHRAVASTI. ONE NIGHT WHEN HE WAS FAST ASLEEP...

...THE ROOM WAS SUDDENLY LIT BY FLASHES OF LIGHT. HE WOKE UP WITH A START.

WHO-WHAT'S THAT? THE WEAPONS! WHAT'S HAPPENING TO THEM? WHY DO THEY GLITTER SO?

\* PART OF MODERN U.P.

THE NEXT MOMENT HOWEVER ALL WAS DARK AGAIN.

WAS IT A NIGHTMARE? WAS MY IMAGINATION PLAYING TRICKS ON ME? OR WAS I REALLY DAZZLED BY THE LIGHT FROM THE WEAPONS?

THE NEXT MORNING, ANY DOUBTS HE MIGHT HAVE HAD, VANISHED.

AT MIDNIGHT, THE WEAPONS IN THE ARMOURY AND IN EVERY HOUSE OF KOSALA, BLAZED, FOR A MOMENT, WITH A BRILLIANT LIGHT.

A STRANGE THING HAPPENED LAST NIGHT, YOUR MAJESTY!

AT THAT MOMENT, IN THE HOUSE OF THE ROYAL PRIEST, GARGA —

HOW HANDSOME IS OUR NEW-BORN SON!

HE IS, NO DOUBT. BUT I AM WORRIED. IMMEDIATELY AFTER HIS BIRTH, STRANGE LIGHTS ISSUED FORTH FROM THE WEAPONS OF THE NIGHT-GUARDS.

LET YOUR SON HAVE A SOUND EDUCATION. UNDER YOUR GUIDANCE, I HAVE NO DOUBT THAT HE WILL GROW UP TO BE A GOOD CITIZEN.

THANK YOU, YOUR MAJESTY. I WILL TRY MY BEST TO INSTIL VIRTUE IN HIM.

THE INFANT WHO WAS NAMED AHIMSAKA, GREW UP TO BE AN INTELLIGENT BOY.

ONE AS DEDICATED AS HE IS TO THE STUDY OF THE SCRIPTURES, CAN NEVER BECOME A ROBBER.

THEN, WHEN AHIMSAKA WAS ABOUT FOURTEEN YEARS OLD—

FATHER, PLEASE, PERMIT ME TO GO TO TAKSHASHILA.*

YOU MAY GO, MY SON. YOU HAVE MY BLESSINGS.

AHIMSAKA LEFT FOR TAKSHASHILA THAT VERY DAY.

ALL THE WAY TO TAKSHASHILA FOR THE SAKE OF LEARNING! HOW CAN AHIMSAKA EVER BECOME A ROBBER? THERE MUST HAVE BEEN SOME MISTAKE IN THE PROPHECY.

* A RENOWNED CENTRE OF LEARNING

ON REACHING TAKSHASHILA, AHIMSAKA WENT TO A GREAT SCHOLAR OF THOSE DAYS.

I, AHIMSAKA, SON OF GARGA OF SHRAVASTI, SALUTE YOU. ACCEPT ME AS YOUR DISCIPLE, MASTER.

YOU ARE WELCOME, MY SON. I WILL TEACH YOU.

AHIMSAKA SOON WON THE HEART OF THE MASTER.

LOOK AT AHIMSAKA. WITHIN SUCH A SHORT TIME, HE HAS MASTERED WHAT YOU COULD NOT IN THE LAST THREE YEARS. HE HAS A GREAT FUTURE BEFORE HIM.

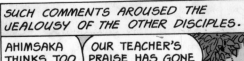

SUCH COMMENTS AROUSED THE JEALOUSY OF THE OTHER DISCIPLES.

AHIMSAKA THINKS TOO MUCH OF HIMSELF.

OUR TEACHER'S PRAISE HAS GONE TO HIS HEAD.

WE MUST DO SOMETHING ABOUT IT.

THEY HATCHED A PLOT TO ESTRANGE THE MASTER FROM HIS FAVOURITE DISCIPLE.

QUICK! THE MASTER IS APPROACHING. LET US BEGIN OUR LITTLE DRAMA.

AHIMSAKA IS A GREAT SCHOLAR.

THAT'S WHY OUR MASTER PRAISES HIM SO.

INDEED, HE IS A GREATER SCHOLAR EVEN THAN OUR MASTER.

AT LEAST THE WIFE OF OUR REVERED MASTER THINKS SO.

THE MASTER BECAME THOUGHTFUL.

PERHAPS THERE IS AN ELEMENT OF TRUTH IN WHAT THE BOYS SAY.

ONE DAY AHIMSAKA MAY PROVE TO BE MORE LEARNED THAN ME. I MUST SEE THAT HE IS MADE AN OUT-CASTE, SHUNNED BY ALL.

WHEN HE ENTERED THE HOUSE —

DOES MY WIFE REALLY THINK HE IS A GREATER SCHOLAR THAN ME? HOW ATTENTIVELY SHE LISTENS TO WHAT HE SAYS! DOES SHE HAVE A GREATER REGARD FOR HIM THAN SHE HAS FOR ME?

WHATEVER THE TRUTH MAY BE, AHIMSAKA WILL HAVE TO GO.

HE ENTERED THE HALL STEALTHILY SO THAT HIS WIFE AND AHIMSAKA, DEEPLY ENGROSSED IN THEIR DISCUSSIONS, WOULD NOT NOTICE HIS PRESENCE.

AHIMSAKA! GET UP!

I HAVE BEEN STANDING HERE ALL THIS WHILE. HAVE YOU BECOME SO ARROGANT THAT YOU FORGET TO ACKNOWLEDGE THE PRESENCE OF YOUR GURU * ?

PARDON ME, MASTER. I...

THE MASTER, HOWEVER, DIDN'T GIVE HIM A CHANCE TO CONTINUE.

HUMILITY SHOULD BE THE OUTCOME OF KNOWLEDGE, NOT ARROGANCE. YOU HAVE NO PLACE HERE. YOU MAY GO.

AS A BEMUSED AHIMSAKA WALKED AWAY FROM THE MASTER'S HOUSE, THE OTHER DISCIPLES GLOATED OVER THE SUCCESS OF THEIR PLOT.

IT WORKED!

I WAS CERTAIN IT WOULD.

WHEN AHIMSAKA RETURNED TO SHRAVASTI —

WHY ARE YOU BACK SO SOON? HAVE YOU FINISHED YOUR STUDIES?

NO, FATHER. I WAS SENT AWAY. I INCURRED THE DISPLEASURE OF MY MASTER. BUT I ...

WHAT! INCURRED THE DISPLEASURE OF YOUR MASTER! DON'T SHOW ME YOUR ACCURSED FACE! GO AWAY FROM HERE!

WHAT HAVE I DONE TO DESERVE SUCH A FATE? WHAT SHALL I DO?

THEY SLAM THEIR DOORS ON MY FACE. WHY MY MASTER SENT ME AWAY, I STILL DO NOT KNOW. FATHER DID NOT EVEN WANT TO HEAR MY STORY.

DEEP IN THOUGHT, AHIMSAKA LEFT KOSALA.

WHAT WAS MY FAULT? WHY HAVE I BEEN TREATED SO CRUELLY? THEY LABEL ME A SINNER. BUT IT IS I WHO HAVE BEEN SINNED AGAINST.

SUDDENLY —

SURRENDER WHATEVER YOU HAVE IF YOU VALUE YOUR LIFE.

NO! NO! NO!

TAKE THIS! AND THIS! THERE! I AM GIVING YOU ALL THAT I HAVE!

MERCY! PLEASE HAVE MERCY ON ME.

DISGUSTED, AHIMSAKA LET HIM GO.

HE HAS SHOWN ME THE WAY. I WILL BE A HIGHWAY ROBBER. I'LL BE MAKING A LIVING WHILE I TAKE REVENGE ON THE SOCIETY THAT REJECTED ME.

LATER, IN THE EVENING, A FLEET OF BULLOCK CARTS CARRYING MERCHANDISE PASSED THAT WAY ON THEIR WAY TO KAUSHAMBI.

HALT!

MY GOD! A ROBBER!

* LITTLE FINGERS

SOON, AHIMSAKA'S ATROCIOUS DEEDS BECAME THE TALK OF KOSALA.

HE IS A MONSTER.

WHO IS HE?

NO ONE KNOWS WHO HE IS NOR WHERE HE COMES FROM.

HE WEARS A STRANGE GARLAND...

SO I'VE HEARD—AN ANGULIMALA! *

AND AHIMSAKA BEGAN TO BE KNOWN AS ANGULIMALA.

THE TRADERS WHO HAD TO TRAVEL, CARRYING MERCHANDISE, WERE THE WORST HIT BY ANGULIMALA, AS THE SHORTEST ROUTE TO KAUSHAMBI WAS THROUGH ANGULIMALA'S HAUNTS.

STOP!

IT'S ANGULIMALA! DRIVE FASTER.

HA, HA! THERE IS NO ESCAPE FROM ME. GET DOWN ALL OF YOU.

* A GARLAND OF LITTLE FINGERS

AS SOON AS THE MERCHANTS WERE MASSACRED BY ANGULIMALA—

COME, MY FRIENDS! THIS FEAST IS FOR YOU.

AHA! HOW DID YOU ESCAPE MY SWORD?

SPARE MY LIFE. HAVE MERCY ON ME.

MERCY? WHAT DOES THAT MEAN?

I WANT TO LIVE FOR THE SAKE OF MY LITTLE SON...

AND I WANT TO KILL YOU FOR YOUR LITTLE FINGER; HA! HA!

AT LAST THE TERROR-STRICKEN SUBJECTS TURNED TO PRASENAJIT.

YOUR MAJESTY, DELIVER US FROM ANGULI-MALA.

I WILL COMMAND MY FOREST GUARDS TO CAPTURE THE NOTORIOUS MURDERER.

AS THE FOREST GUARDS ENTERED ANGULIMALA'S HAUNT —

A WHOLE ARMY OF THEM! GOOD! THAT MANY MORE FINGERS FOR MY GARLAND!

LIFTING UP HUGE BOULDERS, ANGULIMALA HURLED THEM AT THE GUARDS...

...AND THEN SPRANG UPON THEM.

A FEW, HOWEVER, WERE ABLE TO ESCAPE WITH THEIR LIVES.

WHEN THEY REPORTED TO PRASENAJIT —

JUST ONE MAN, AND YOU WERE HELPLESS AGAINST HIM!

THAT EVENING, THE ROYAL DRUMMER WENT ROUND THE CITY.

GIVE EAR! GIVE EAR! PEOPLE ARE ADVISED TO AVOID ANGULIMALA. THOSE GOING TO KAUSHAMBI SHOULD TAKE THE ROUTE VIA MAGADHA...

ANGULIMALA WAITED IN VAIN FOR VICTIMS.

MY GARLAND HAS BEGUN TO WITHER. I NEED NEW FINGERS! I WISH SOMEONE WOULD PASS THIS WAY.

SUDDENLY HE SPOTTED A MONK WALKING BY.

MY PRAYER HAS BEEN HEARD!

HALT!

ANGULIMALA RAN AFTER THE MONK.

TO HIS ASTONISHMENT, HOWEVER, THE MONK, WHO SEEMED TO BE WALKING AT A LEISURELY PACE, WAS ALWAYS A STEP AHEAD.

AT LAST EXHAUSTED BY THE CHASE, ANGULIMALA PAUSED.

O MONK, STOP! STOP MOVING.

I AM NOT MOVING. I AM AT REST. IT IS YOU WHO ARE IN PERPETUAL MOTION.

ANGULIMALA COLLAPSED AT THE FEET OF THE MONK.

GET UP, MY CHILD.

MASTER!

MASTER, HENCEFORTH I WILL NEVER KILL.

THE MONK BROUGHT HIM TO THE MONASTERY ON THE OUTSKIRTS OF SHRAVASTI.

SALUTATIONS TO YOU, MY MASTER.

ANATHAPINDIKA, I HAVE BROUGHT YET ANOTHER BROTHER—ANGULIMALA.

THE LOVING MONK WAS NONE OTHER THAN LORD BUDDHA.

20

THE NEXT MORNING, PRASENAJIT VISITED THE MONASTERY. THE KING HAD COME TO PAY HIS RESPECTS TO THE MASTER.

IT LOOKS AS THOUGH YOU HAVE STARTED ON AN EXPEDITION.

YES, MASTER. I WANT TO EXTERMINATE THAT MONSTER—ANGULIMALA. I HAVE COME FOR YOUR BLESSINGS.

SUPPOSING ANGULIMALA GIVES UP THE PATH OF VIOLENCE AND BEGINS TO LIVE THE LIFE OF AN ASCETIC, WHAT WILL YOUR REACTION BE?

I WILL SALUTE HIM THEN, MY LORD. BUT PARDON ME, I CAN'T IMAGINE ANGULIMALA AS AN ASCETIC.

BUT HE HAS BECOME ONE. THERE HE IS, WATERING THE PLANTS.

WHAT!

21

I COULD NOT SUBDUE ANGULI-MALA WITH ALL MY STRENGTH AND YOU HAVE WON HIM WITHOUT LIFTING YOUR LITTLE FINGER. WE ARE GRATEFUL TO YOU, LORD.

THEN, SALUTING ANGULIMALA, THE KING LEFT.

ANGULIMALA BECAME DEVOTED TO BUDDHA. HE LISTENED TO THE MASTER'S WORDS OF WISDOM.

HE NURSED THE SICK.

I AM FEELING BETTER NOW, ANGULIMALA. YOU MAY REST.

DON'T MIND ME, BROTHER. YOU SLEEP.

ONE DAY WHEN ANGULIMALA WENT TO BEG FOR HIS FOOD.

DO YOU WANT MORE RICE?

YOU ARE GENEROUS, MY CHILD. MAY YOU, YOUR MOTHER AND FATHER BE BLESSED.

I HAVE NO FATHER. HE IS DEAD. HE WAS KILLED BY THE WICKED ANGULI-MALA.

OH!

SICK AT HEART, ANGULIMALA WALKED BACK TO THE MONASTERY...

...WHERE HE SPENT MANY A SLEEPLESS NIGHT.

I AM AN ORPHAN. YOU MADE ME ONE!

MURDERER!

YOU KILLED MY FATHER.

OH! NO, NO!

YES, YOU ARE A MURDERER!

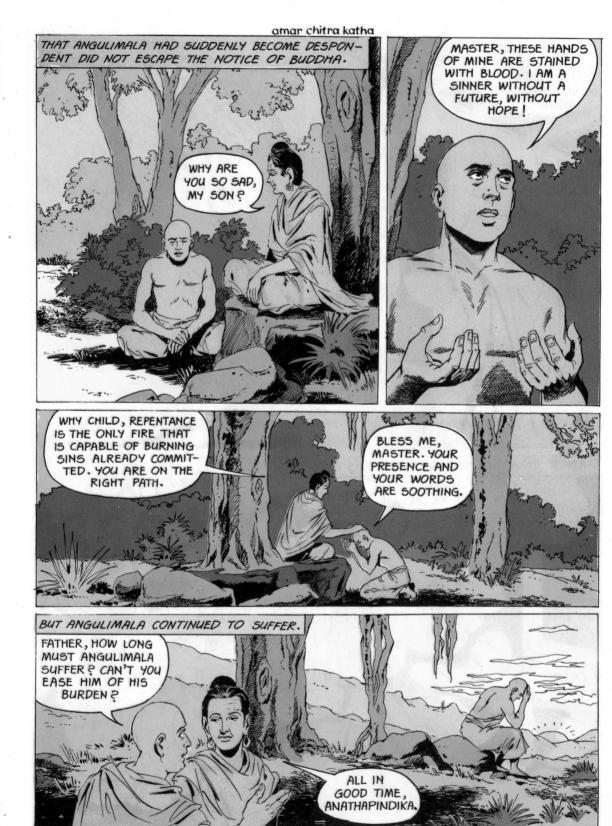

THAT ANGULIMALA HAD SUDDENLY BECOME DESPONDENT DID NOT ESCAPE THE NOTICE OF BUDDHA.

WHY ARE YOU SO SAD, MY SON?

MASTER, THESE HANDS OF MINE ARE STAINED WITH BLOOD. I AM A SINNER WITHOUT A FUTURE, WITHOUT HOPE!

WHY CHILD, REPENTANCE IS THE ONLY FIRE THAT IS CAPABLE OF BURNING SINS ALREADY COMMITTED. YOU ARE ON THE RIGHT PATH.

BLESS ME, MASTER. YOUR PRESENCE AND YOUR WORDS ARE SOOTHING.

BUT ANGULIMALA CONTINUED TO SUFFER.

FATHER, HOW LONG MUST ANGULIMALA SUFFER? CAN'T YOU EASE HIM OF HIS BURDEN?

ALL IN GOOD TIME, ANATHAPINDIKA.

24

THEN ONE DAY, BUDDHA TOOK ANGULIMALA WITH HIM ON HIS ROUNDS. AS THEY PROCEEDED—

OH, GOD! I CAN'T BEAR IT...AH!... OOH!...

MASTER, SOMEONE SEEMS TO BE IN PAIN. LET US HURRY.

WHAT'S THE TROUBLE, MOTHER?

MY DAUGHTER IS ABOUT TO DELIVER A BABY, SIR. WE WERE ON OUR WAY TO TOWN.

CAN'T YOU ALLEVIATE HER MISERY, MASTER?

MOTHER, I AM DYING.

MY SON, BLESS THE WOMAN AND SAY: "WHEN I KILLED PEOPLE, I DID SO OUT OF IGNORANCE. IF I SPEAK THE TRUTH, LET THE WOMAN GET WELL."

BUT MASTER...

OH, SIR, DON'T SAY NO! PLEASE DON'T! SAVE HER.

WITH MUCH RELUCTANCE, ANGULIMALA OBEYED HIS MASTER'S ORDERS.

HOW CAN I, A RUTHLESS MURDERER, SAVE HER?

I DON'T KNOW IF I HAD KILLED WITH FULL KNOWLEDGE. IF I AM CORRECT IN SAYING SO, LET THIS WOMAN GET WELL.

AND THE TWO RESUMED THEIR JOURNEY. SUDDENLY —

OH, SIR, PLEASE WAIT.

IT'S THE OLD WOMAN. HER DAUGHTER MUST BE DYING.

THE OLD WOMAN APPEARED, BRINGING NEWS NOT OF DEATH, BUT OF LIFE.

SIR, YOU BLESSED MY DAUGHTER AND SAVED HER LIFE. BLESS HER LITTLE SON, TOO.

MOTHER, MERCIFUL BUDDHA WILL BLESS HIM.

I WANT BOTH OF YOU TO BLESS THE CHILD.

THE MASTER AND THE DISCIPLE BLESSED THE CHILD.

WHEN THE OLD WOMAN WENT AWAY—

ANGULIMALA, AT LEAST NOW ARE YOU CONVINCED THAT YOU HAVE OVERCOME YOUR PAST DEEDS?

I AM, MASTER, THANKS TO YOU.

SON, YOU NO LONGER NEED ME. YOU MUST WALK ALONE IN THE WORLD.

IF YOU INSIST, I WILL. BUT IT IS YOU WHO HAVE GIVEN ME THE STRENGTH TO DO SO. BUDDHAM SHARANAM GACCHAMI.*

AFTER PARTING FROM BUDDHA, ANGULIMALA DECIDED TO GO TO SHRAVASTI. AS HE ENTERED THE CITY—

LOOK! DID YOU RECOGNISE HIM?

WHY? HE IS JUST A COMMON MONK. OR IS HE A GREAT ONE?

* I TAKE REFUGE IN BUDDHA

YOU FOOL, HE IS NONE OTHER THAN ANGULI-MALA IN DISGUISE.

ANGULIMALA? HAS HE COME HERE BECAUSE PEOPLE NO LONGER PASS BY HIS HAUNTS? GOD HELP US!

THE NEWS SPREAD AND PEOPLE BEGAN TO PANIC.

ANGULIMALA IS COMING!

ANGULIMALA! RUN!

RUN FOR YOUR LIVES!

BUT SOME YOUNGSTERS MUSTERED UP THEIR COURAGE.

NO, WE SHALL NOT RUN AWAY. COME, WE WILL KILL HIM BEFORE HE KILLS US ALL.

YES, WE WILL KILL HIM.

ARMING THEMSELVES, A FURIOUS MOB APPROACHED ANGULIMALA.

LOOK! A CHILD HAS COME OUT TO OFFER RICE TO THE MONSTER IN DISGUISE.

HE IS GOING TO STRANGLE THAT CHILD.

NO, HE IS KISSING IT! STRANGE!

AS SOON AS ANGULIMALA STEPPED OUT OF THE HOUSE, A STONE HIT HIM ON THE FOREHEAD.

IT WAS FOLLOWED BY MANY MORE.

THEN THE MOB LET LOOSE ITS PENT-UP FURY.

HIT HIM HARD!

GIVE ME A CHANCE. IT'S MY TURN NOW.

WHAT DOES IT FEEL LIKE? WHY DON'T YOU FIGHT BACK?

BUT ANGULIMALA DID NOT RAISE A FINGER TO PROTECT HIMSELF.

SEVERLY BEATEN UP, HE STARTED CRAWLING TOWARDS THE ABODE OF HIS MASTER.

MAY YOU DIE A DOG'S DEATH.

WHEN HE REACHED THE MONASTERY—

ANGULIMALA, MY CHILD!

BUDDHAM... SHARANAM.. GA..CCHAA..MI.*

*I TAKE REFUGE IN BUDDHA

AND ANGULIMALA BREATHED HIS LAST.

# AMRAPALI

## CHOSEN BY BUDDHA

www.amarchitrakatha.com

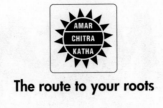

**The route to your roots**

# AMRAPALI

This collection of Buddhist tales tell of Amrapali, an accomplished dancer who commanded the love and admiration of an entire town, and of Upagupta, who was just a poor monk. Amrapali craved peace; Upagupta's bearing exuded contentment. Amrapali depended on the adulation of her audience; Upagupta spurned the attentions of the rich and famous. Their stories were different, but the Buddha's wise teachings linked their lives – and the lessons to be learned from them.

| **Script** | **Illustrations** | **Editor** |
|:---:|:---:|:---:|
| Subba Rao | H.S.Chavan & Ranjana | Anant Pai |

*Cover illustration by: C.M.Vitankar*

# AMRAPALI

THE LICCHAVI NOBLES, WHO RULED OVER ANCIENT VAISHALI, WERE GREAT LOVERS OF BEAUTY AND TOOK A KEEN INTEREST IN THE MAINTENANCE OF THEIR GARDENS.

THE BEST OF GARDENERS WAS EMPLOYED TO TEND THE PLANTS.

ONE DAY —

WHAT'S THAT UNDER THE MANGO TREE? WHY, IT'S A LADY! WHAT AN EXTRA-ORDINARY BEAUTY!

1

HE WENT UP TO HER.

WHO ARE YOU, FAIR LADY? WHAT IS YOUR NAME? WHERE HAVE YOU COME FROM? AND WHAT IS YOUR DESTINATION?

I DON'T HAVE A NAME. I COME FROM NOWHERE AND HAVE NOWHERE TO GO.

ARE YOU GOING TO LIVE IN THIS GARDEN?

YES. IF YOU DO NOT MIND, I WOULD LIKE TO LIVE HERE.

I CERTAINLY DON'T MIND. BUT THIS GARDEN BELONGS TO THE NOBLES. THEY SHOULD BE INFORMED.

WHEN THEY REACHED THE GARDEN —

THE GARDENER KNEW WHAT HE WAS TALKING ABOUT! SHE IS THE MOST ENCHANTING LADY I HAVE EVER SEEN!

AMRAPALI* SHALL BE MINE!

YOU'LL HAVE TO TAKE HER FROM ME FIRST!

A FIERCE FIGHT BROKE OUT AMONG THE NOBLES. EACH WANTED AMRAPALI FOR HIMSELF!

* THE MANGO-GIRL, AS SHE WAS FOUND NEAR THE MANGO TREE

4

THE ELDERS OF VAISHALI, WHO HAD HURRIED TO THE GARDEN ON HEARING THE CLASH, SUPPORTED HER.

A WISE DECISION, INDEED! AMRAPALI CANNOT BELONG TO ONE PERSON. SHE SHALL BELONG TO VAISHALI.

WE AGREE.

AMRAPALI HAS NO PLACE TO LIVE IN. LET US PRESENT THIS GARDEN TO HER.

AND WE COULD HAVE A HOUSE BUILT HERE FOR HER.

AS SOON AS THE HOUSE WAS READY —

THIS GARDEN AND THE HOUSE ARE YOURS, AMRAPALI.

I SHALL EVER REMAIN INDEBTED TO THE PEOPLE OF VAISHALI FOR THE LOVE THEY HAVE SHOWN ME.

TO ENTERTAIN THE NOBLES OF VAISHALI, AMRAPALI, AN EXCELLENT DANCER, BEGAN TO GIVE DANCE PERFORMANCES.

SUCH PERFECT RHYTHM!

SHE IS MATCHLESS!

NO OTHER KINGDOM CAN BOAST OF SUCH AN ACCOMPLISHED DANCER!

SHE IS INDEED, THE PRIDE OF VAISHALI!

ONE EVENING, WHEN THE NOBLES WERE WATCHING AMRAPALI PERFORM, A MESSENGER RUSHED IN.

MASTER! I HAVE BAD NEWS! VAISHALI IS IN DANGER!

THE STRANGER STAYED WITH HER FOR A WEEK. THEN —

AMRAPALI, I MUST TAKE YOUR LEAVE. I HAVE TO GO BACK.

I LOVE YOU, AMRAPALI. WHY DON'T YOU COME AWAY WITH ME?

YOU AMUSE ME. YOU ARE A TOTAL STRANGER. I DON'T EVEN KNOW YOUR NAME!

I AM BIMBISARA.

WHAT! THE DREADED KING OF MAGADHA!

THERE IS NO ROOM FOR LOVE IN THE HEARTS OF AMBITIOUS MEN! HOW CAN YOU TALK OF LOVE, WHEN THIS VERY MOMENT BECAUSE OF YOU HUNDREDS OF MEN ARE DYING ON THE BATTLEFIELD?

IF I GIVE UP MY AMBITION TO CONQUER VAISHALI AND CEASE HOSTILITIES FORTH-WITH, WILL YOU MARRY ME?

NO! I CANNOT!

WHY NOT, AMRAPALI? DON'T YOU LOVE ME?

I BELONG TO VAISHALI! I HAVE GIVEN MY PLEDGE.

WITHOUT ANOTHER WORD, THE DEJECTED BIMBISARA TURNED AND LEFT. AMRAPALI COULD NOT UNDERSTAND HER OWN FEELINGS.

WHY DO I FEEL SAD TO SEE THE DREADED ENEMY OF VAISHALI GO?

A FEW DAYS LATER —

AMRAPALI, WE ARE BACK.

THAT COWARD, BIMBISARA, CALLED OFF THE BATTLE.

WHY DID HE DO IT? WAS IT FOR LOVE OF ME?

AMRAPALI, WE MISSED YOU.

WE WOULD LIKE TO SEE YOU COMPLETE THE DANCE YOU BEGAN, WHEN WE LEFT.

YOU SHALL, IN A MOMENT.

AS AMRAPALI DANCED —

WHAT IS WRONG WITH HER TODAY?

HER MOVEMENTS ARE LIFELESS.

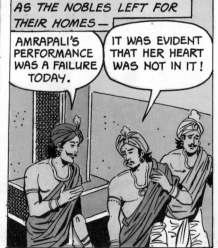

AS THE NOBLES LEFT FOR THEIR HOMES —

AMRAPALI'S PERFORMANCE WAS A FAILURE TODAY.

IT WAS EVIDENT THAT HER HEART WAS NOT IN IT!

13

HAVEN'T YOU HEARD? LORD BUDDHA HAS COME TO VAISHALI AND IS CAMPING AT KOTIGRAMA. I AM TAKING THIS FLOWER TO HIM.

AS THE BOY WENT HIS WAY—

LORD BUDDHA! THE ENLIGHTENED ONE WHO KNOWS THE CAUSE OF SUFFERING! I WILL GO TO HIM.

SHE WENT TO KOTIGRAMA.

SHE LISTENED TO LORD BUDDHA WITH RAPT ATTENTION.

OUT OF DESIRE IS BORN GRIEF. OUT OF DESIRE ALONE IS BORN FEAR. FREE YOURSELF FROM DESIRE AND THE GRIEF AND THE FEAR WILL WITHER AWAY.

SHE BEGAN TO EXPERIENCE A NEW KIND OF JOY.

HIS WORDS FILL ME WITH PEACE! HIS VOICE IS SO SOFT! HIS WORDS SO SOOTHING!

SHE WENT TO KOTIGRAMA DAILY. ONE DAY —

HIS VERY PRESENCE STILLS MY RESTLESS MIND. HOW I WISH HE WOULD VISIT MY HOME AND FILL IT WITH HIS BEING!

BUT WILL THE LORD VISIT THE HOUSE OF AN UNWORTHY PERSON LIKE ME?

SOON IT WAS TIME FOR LORD BUDDHA TO LEAVE VAISHALI.

WHEN WILL I SEE YOU AGAIN, MASTER?

EVEN AFTER LORD BUDDHA HAD LEFT, AMRAPALI CONTINUED TO VISIT KOTIGRAMA EVERY EVENING.

THIS IS WHERE THE MASTER USED TO SIT. I CAN STILL FEEL HIS PRESENCE HERE.

MANY MONTHS PASSED. AND AMRAPALI PATIENTLY WAITED FOR THE RETURN OF LORD BUDDHA.

MY MASTER WILL COME TO VAISHALI AGAIN. PERHAPS TODAY, PERHAPS TOMORROW, BUT HE WILL COME.

ONE EVENING —

MY MASTER IS BACK!! I CAN'T BELIEVE MY EYES.

SHE RAN UP TO LORD BUDDHA AND FELL AT HIS FEET.

ARISE, MY CHILD.

AND BEFORE SHE COULD STOP HERSELF, THE WORDS POURED OUT.

MASTER, WILL YOU HONOUR ME BY EATING AT MY HOUSE TOMORROW?

I WILL COME, MY CHILD.

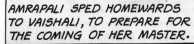

AMRAPALI SPED HOMEWARDS TO VAISHALI, TO PREPARE FOR THE COMING OF HER MASTER.

17

SUDDENLY, A FEW CHARIOTS CARRYING THE NOBLES OF VAISHALI, CAME CHARGING FROM THE OPPOSITE DIRECTION.

WHERE ARE YOU SPEEDING TO?

WE HEARD THAT LORD BUDDHA HAS ARRIVED. WE ARE OFF TO INVITE HIM TO EAT WITH US AT THE PALACE TOMORROW.

BUT THE LORD HAS ALREADY AGREED TO DINE AT MY HOUSE TOMORROW.

WE HAVE BEEN FORESTALLED!

NOT ALL IS LOST. NOT YET. SHE CAN EASILY BE BOUGHT OFF.

AMRAPALI, IF YOU LET LORD BUDDHA HAVE HIS FIRST MEAL AT VAISHALI WITH US, WE WILL GIVE YOU ALL THE GOLD YOU WANT.

NO. EVEN IF YOU OFFER ME THE KINGDOM OF VAISHALI, I WON'T GIVE UP THE HONOUR OF SERVING THE LORD!

AS AMRAPALI DROVE AWAY —

WHAT SHALL WE DO?

WE WILL GO TO THE LORD. HE CANNOT REFUSE THE NOBLES OF VAISHALI.

LATER, AT KOTIGRAMA —

LORD, PLEASE HONOUR US BY DINING WITH US TOMORROW.

I AM SORRY. I CAN'T. I HAVE ALREADY AGREED TO GO TO AMRAPALI'S HOUSE TOMORROW.

THE NEXT DAY, LORD BUDDHA WENT TO AMRAPALI'S HOUSE.

I HAVE COME, AMRAPALI.

LORD, YOU DO ME GREAT HONOUR.

LATER —

LORD, WHY DO I FEEL SUCH IMMENSE JOY AS I SERVE YOU?

AMRAPALI, YOU HAVE BEGUN TO KNOW THE JOY OF GIVING.

LATER —

LORD, PERMIT ME TO GRANT MY GARDEN AND HOUSE TO THE SANGHA.

SO BE IT, CHILD. IT COULD BE USED AS A MONASTERY.

THEN, LEAVING BEHIND HER THE WORLDLY LIFE AND ITS HEARTACHES...

...AMRAPALI BEGAN TO LEAD A LIFE OF RENUNCIATION, FINDING AT LAST THE PEACE OF MIND SHE HAD CRAVED.

# UPAGUPTA

LONG, LONG AGO IN ANCIENT MATHURA, THERE LIVED A DANCER CALLED VASAVADATTA, WHO WAS FAMED FOR HER BEAUTY AND HER ART.

WHAT A PERFECT FIGURE! WHAT A CHARMING APPEARANCE! WHAT GRACEFUL MOVEMENTS...

...AND WHAT A HARD HEART! SHE'S UNIQUE, INDEED!

YOU SEEM BITTER. HAVE YOU TOO BEEN SPURNED BY HER?

AFTER THE PERFORMANCE, AS VASAVADATTA LEFT THE TOWN HALL —

I AM PREPARED TO PART WITH ALL MY WEALTH FOR A SMILE FROM HER.

WITH NOT SO MUCH AS A GLANCE AT HER ADMIRERS, VASAVADATTA SAT IN HER CHARIOT AND RODE HOME WITH HER COMPANION.

THEY ARE ALL MADLY IN LOVE WITH YOU. COULDN'T YOU SEE IT IN THEIR EYES?

I CHOSE NOT TO SEE.

WHY, VASAVADATTA? WHY DON'T YOU MARRY ONE OF THEM? IS THERE NOT A SINGLE ONE WHOM YOU DEEM WORTHY OF YOUR LOVE?

NO! NOT ONE OF THEM POSSESSES WHAT I AM LOOKING FOR.

ONE EVENING, AS VASAVADATTA WAS STANDING IN THE BALCONY OF HER MANSION, SHE SAW A YOUNG MONK PASS BY IN THE STREET BELOW.

QUICK! RUN DOWN AND INVITE THAT MONK IN.

I CAN'T BELIEVE IT. VASAVADATTA SHOWING SOME INTEREST IN A MAN!

VASAVADATTA WISHES TO SEE YOU, HOLY ONE. WILL YOU COME IN?

NOT NOW. I WILL SEE HER AT THE PROPER TIME.

THE MONK WHO SPURNED THE INVITATION OF THE DANCER, WAS UPAGUPTA, A DISCIPLE OF LORD BUDDHA.

WHEN VASAVADATTA WAS TOLD OF THE MONK'S REACTION —

PERHAPS, HE HESITATES TO VISIT ME BECAUSE HE IS POOR AND CAN'T BRING ME GIFTS. TELL HIM I DON'T WANT ANYTHING FROM HIM.

HER FRIEND WENT BACK TO UPAGUPTA.

O MONK, MY FRIEND DOES NOT CRAVE FOR GIFTS OR RICHES. PLEASE VISIT HER.

NO, I CANNOT. IT IS NOT YET TIME TO VISIT VASAVADATTA.

AND UPAGUPTA WALKED AWAY.

VASAVADATTA WAS STUNNED.

WHY SHOULD THE ONLY MAN I CHOOSE TO LOVE, SHUN ME?

SHE STOPPED GIVING DANCE PERFORMANCES, MUCH TO THE ANNOYANCE OF THE PEOPLE OF MATHURA.

WHAT IS THE MATTER WITH VASAVADATTA?

LIFE IN MATHURA HAS LOST ITS CHARM. HOW COULD SHE BE SO CRUEL TO US!

MEANWHILE, HER FRIEND WAS WORRIED.

SHE SITS ALONE, BROODING OVER THAT HEARTLESS MONK. IT IS NOT GOOD FOR HER HEALTH AND LOOKS. I MUST FIND SOMETHING TO DISTRACT HER.

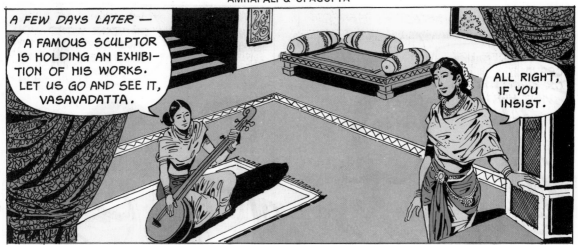

A FEW DAYS LATER —

A FAMOUS SCULPTOR IS HOLDING AN EXHIBITION OF HIS WORKS. LET US GO AND SEE IT, VASAVADATTA.

ALL RIGHT, IF YOU INSIST.

AT THE SHOW, VASAVADATTA FORGOT HER SORROW FOR A WHILE.

SUCH EXQUISITE WORKMANSHIP!

WILL YOU SELL THIS TO ME?

YOU MIGHT FIND THE PRICE TOO HEAVY.

WHATEVER IT MAY COST, I AM PREPARED TO BUY IT. QUOTE YOUR PRICE.

IT'S YOURS, IF YOU AGREE TO DANCE AGAIN.

VASAVADATTA HESITATED —

TO... DANCE...

YOU CAN'T GO BACK ON YOUR WORD. YOU HAVE AGREED TO PAY WHATEVER PRICE HE ASKS.

VASAVADATTA RELUCTANTLY AGREED.

THE NEXT EVENING, PEOPLE FLOCKED TO THE TOWN HALL.

AT LAST WE WILL SEE VASAVA-DATTA DANCE AGAIN!

THANKS TO THE CHIEF SCULPTOR OF OUR CITY. IT WAS INDEED A CLEVER BARGAIN!

AT THE END OF THE PERFORMANCE, VASAVADATTA RECEIVED THUNDEROUS APPLAUSE. BUT INSTEAD OF MAKING HER HAPPY, IT ONLY MADE HER BROOD ALL THE MORE.

WHY DID THAT MONK SHUN ME WHEN THOUSANDS OF PEOPLE LONG FOR A SIGHT OF ME?

IN THE DAYS THAT FOLLOWED, THE CHIEF SCULPTOR BEGAN TO VISIT THE DANCER TO CAPTURE HER IMAGE IN STONE.

MY ART WILL DIE WITH ME. BUT YOURS WILL LAST FOR CENTURIES.

MY TALENT, WHICH BRINGS SO MUCH HAPPINESS TO YOU, ONLY MAKES MY ENVIOUS RIVALS HATE ME.

A FEW DAYS LATER, THE SCULPTOR SUDDENLY VANISHED.

WHY DOESN'T HE COME? THE WORK IS YET TO BE COMPLETED. IT'S THREE DAYS SINCE HE LAST CAME!

PERHAPS HE IS OUT OF TOWN.

MEANWHILE, HIS FRIENDS AND RELATIVES TOO WERE SEARCHING FOR THE CHIEF SCULPTOR.

HAVE HIS RIVALS DONE AWAY WITH HIM?

HE WAS LAST SEEN ENTERING THE HOUSE OF VASAVADATTA, THREE DAYS AGO.

LATER, THE BODY OF THE MISSING SCULPTOR WAS FOUND BURIED NOT FAR FROM VASAVADATTA'S HOUSE. SHE WAS CHARGED WITH THE MURDER OF THE SCULPTOR.

DO YOU HAVE ANYTHING TO SAY IN YOUR DEFENCE?

VASAVADATTA HAD NOTHING TO SAY.

VASAVADATTA IS GUILTY. CONFISCATE HER PROPERTY AND HAVE HER BANISHED FROM MATHURA.

AS VASAVADATTA WAS TURNED OUT OF HER HOUSE, AN ANGRY MOB JEERED AT HER AND PELTED HER WITH STONES.

TAKE THIS, YOU MURDERESS.

SEE THAT YOU NEVER DARKEN OUR CITY AGAIN!

BLEEDING PROFUSELY, VASAVADATTA REACHED THE OUTSKIRTS OF MATHURA AND FOUND REFUGE IN A CREMATORIUM.

VASAVADATTA, I KNOW YOU ARE INNOCENT! THEY HAVE DELIBERATELY DONE THIS TO YOU.

FRIEND, LET US NOT BLAME ANYONE.

PEOPLE COMING IN AND OUT OF MATHURA, LOOKED UPON VASAVADATTA, NOW SERIOUSLY ILL WITH FESTERING WOUNDS, AS AN UNTOUCHABLE.

SHE DOESN'T DESERVE ANY SYMPATHY.

LEAVE HER TO DIE. WHY DO YOU WASTE YOUR TIME ON HER?

THEY WOULD SPIT AT HER AND SOMETIMES EVEN STONE HER AS THEY PASSED BY.

THEN CAME UPAGUPTA, THE BUDDHIST MONK.

FRIEND, COVER MY BODY. LET HIM NOT SEE ME IN THIS STATE.

VASAVADATTA, I HAVE COME TO YOU.

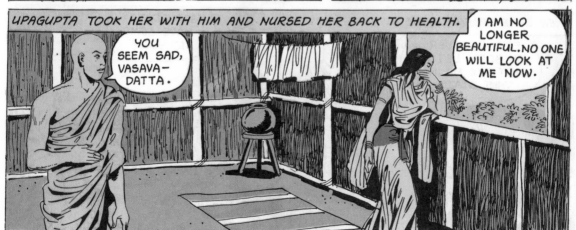

31

# THE ACROBAT

## A COLLECTION OF BUDDHIST TALES

**The route to your roots**

# THE ACROBAT

A talented acrobat, a hard-working farmer, a love-lorn youth and a distraught mother all have something in common. Their lives are affected by Gautam Buddha. He comes to each one of them when the time is right and touches their hearts and minds in such a way that their troubles cease to exist and they are completely at peace.

| **Script** | **Illustrations** | **Editor** |
| Gayatri Madan Dutt | Dilip Kadam | Anant Pai |

CROWDS GATHERED...

...AND THOSE AT THE VERY BACK STOOD ON THEIR TOES TO GET A BETTER VIEW.

LET THE SHOW BEGIN.

3

UGRASENA WENT HOME AND FLUNG HIMSELF ON HIS BED. FATHER, MOTHER—I WANT TO MARRY THE ACROBAT WE SAW TODAY. IF I CAN'T MARRY HER, I SHALL STARVE MYSELF TO DEATH.

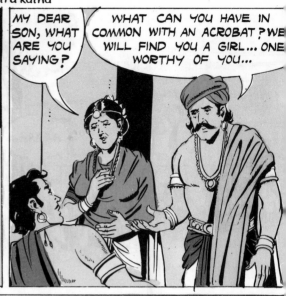

MY DEAR SON, WHAT ARE YOU SAYING?

WHAT CAN YOU HAVE IN COMMON WITH AN ACROBAT? WE WILL FIND YOU A GIRL... ONE WORTHY OF YOU...

IT'S HER OR NONE! I SHALL NOT EVEN LOOK AT ANOTHER GIRL.

THE HELPLESS TREASURER AND HIS WIFE SENT UGRASENA'S FRIEND TO THE ACROBAT'S FATHER. MY FRIEND WISHES TO MARRY YOUR DAUGHTER. AS A MARRIAGE PORTION, HERE IS ALL THE GOLD YOU MIGHT DESIRE.

FOR SHAME! ARE YOU ASKING ME TO SELL MY DAUGHTER?

IF YOUR FRIEND IS WILLING TO TRAVEL WITH US, WHEREVER WE GO, HE MAY MARRY HER.

THE TREASURER AND HIS WIFE WERE SHOCKED TO HEAR THIS.

SON, SURELY YOU WILL NOT LEAVE US TO GO TRAVELLING WITH AN ACROBAT!

I WILL, FOR SHE MEANS EVERYTHING TO ME NOW.

SO UGRASENA MARRIED THE ACROBAT...

...AND JOINED THE TROUPE.

BEING THE ONLY MEMBER OF THE TROUPE UNSKILLED IN ACROBATICS, HE MADE HIMSELF USEFUL IN OTHER WAYS...

...AND WAS CONTENT WITH HIS SIMPLE LIFE.

SOON, A SON WAS BORN TO THEM.

HIS WIFE SPENT ALL HER TIME BETWEEN SHOWS WITH THE BABY.

I'LL ROCK YOU IN MY ARMS, O SON OF A WOOD-FETCHER.

CLOSE YOUR EYES AND SLEEP, O SON OF A WATER-CARRIER.

LET THE JOLT OF THE CART ROCK YOU TO SLEEP, O SON OF A CART-DRIVER.

WOMAN, ARE YOU REFERRING TO ME, WHEN YOU SING THOSE SONGS?

YES... I AM.

YOU ARE TRIFLING WITH ME. I SHALL LEAVE YOU, AND GO AWAY.

DO AS YOU THINK BEST.

IT... IT'S HER SKILL AS AN ACROBAT THAT MAKES HER SO BOLD... SO VAIN... SO INDIFFERENT!

UGRASENA WENT TO HIS FATHER-IN-LAW.

I WANT TO BECOME AN ACROBAT.

I'LL TEACH YOU THE SKILLS.

UGRASENA MADE RAPID PROGRESS IN HIS NEW PROFESSION AND SOON —

I PRESENT BEFORE YOU A NEW PERFORMER — MY SON-IN-LAW.

WHEN UGRASENA DISPLAYED HIS FEATS —

LOOK — HE HAS TURNED SEVEN SOMERSAULTS! UNBELIEVABLE!

HIS WIFE CAN TURN ONLY FOUR!

SOON AT RAJAGRIHA, NEWS SPREAD THAT THE ACROBATS WERE RETURNING AND, WITH THEM, THE TREASURER'S SON.

IT SEEMS UGRASENA WILL PERFORM THE FEAT OF TURNING FOURTEEN SOMERSAULTS IN THE AIR!

IMPOSSIBLE! YOU ARE JOKING!

ON THE APPOINTED DAY, THE ENTIRE CITY GATHERED IN THE SQUARE TO WATCH UGRASENA PERFORM.

JUST AS HE TURNED THE FIRST SOMERSAULT—

LOOK! THE HOLY TEACHER!

8

# THE HARVEST

WATER MY FIELD, O CLOUD WITH YOUR GENTLE RAIN; RIPEN MY CROPS, O SUN, INTO GOLDEN GRAIN...

ONCE A FARMER WAS AT WORK IN HIS FIELD WHEN BUDDHA CAME BY.

AH! WHAT A FINE HARVEST I WILL REAP!

WHAT ARE YOU DOING, O FARMER?

I AM CLEARING MY FIELD, SIR.

THE NEXT DAY, BUDDHA CAME THAT WAY AGAIN.

WHAT ARE YOU BUSY WITH NOW, O FARMER?

I AM PLOUGHING MY FIELD, SIR.

ON EVERY SUCCEEDING DAY AFTER THIS, BUDDHA CAME AND INQUIRED ABOUT THE FARMER'S WORK.

THEN ONE DAY— SIR, I FIND THAT FROM THE DAY I BEGAN TO CLEAR MY FIELD, YOU HAVE BEEN SHOWING A GREAT DEAL OF INTEREST IN MY WORK.

SO WHEN MY CROP IS HARVESTED, I AM GOING TO SHARE IT WITH YOU.

FOR, YOU ARE NOW MY PARTNER.

THE DAYS PASSED AND THE FARMER'S CROPS RIPENED.

I SHALL CALL IN THE REAPERS TOMORROW.

BUT THAT NIGHT, BLACK CLOUDS GATHERED...

...THUNDER AND LIGHTNING RENT THE SKY...

...AND A RAGING STORM BROKE OUT.

THE NEXT MORNING, WHEN THE FARMER HURRIED TO HIS FIELD —

OH, GOD— NO! I AM RUINED!

AND I HAVE PROMISED A SHARE TO MY PARTNER!

THE GRIEF-STRICKEN FARMER RETURNED HOME AND TOOK TO HIS BED.

MASTER, JUST A MOUTHFUL OF FOOD...

NO— TAKE IT AWAY. I WILL NOT EAT.

JUST THEN, BUDDHA ARRIVED THERE.

O FARMER, I WISH TO SPEAK TO YOU.

THE FARMER SLOWLY ROSE AND CAME TO SIT BY BUDDHA.

TELL ME WHY YOU GRIEVE, O FARMER.

LAST NIGHT'S STORM DESTROYED MY CROP...

...AND I CANNOT KEEP MY WORD TO YOU.

YOU WOULD NOT GRIEVE THUS, IF YOU KNEW WHAT YOUR SORROW SPRINGS FROM. IT IS FROM ATTACHMENT, O FARMER.

ATTACHMENT TO YOUR CROPS, TO YOUR WORD, AND TO ME! FROM ATTACHMENT SPRINGS SORROW, FROM ATTACHMENT SPRINGS FEAR.

HE WHO IS FREE FROM ATTACHMENT IS FREE OF THE BURDEN OF BOTH SORROW AND FEAR.

I HAVE UNDERSTOOD, O VENERABLE ONE.

# THE GOLDEN MAIDEN

IN THE TOWN OF SRAVASTI LIVED YOUNG KUMARA. HE WAS THE SON OF RICH PARENTS AND HE HAD COME OF AGE.

SON, YOU ARE OLD ENOUGH TO BE MARRIED. WE SHALL CHOOSE A GOOD, BEAUTIFUL GIRL FOR YOU AND...

FATHER, I DON'T WANT TO GET MARRIED.

BUT THE OLD COUPLE DID NOT GIVE UP. EVERY ONCE IN A WAY, THEY PUT THE QUESTION TO HIM AGAIN. AT LAST...

THEY WILL NOT TAKE 'NO' FOR AN ANSWER.

THE ONLY WAY OUT IS TO AGREE BUT MAKE SURE THAT THEY WON'T FIND THE GIRL FOR ME.

THE YOUNG MAN GOT SKILLED ARTISANS TO CARVE A GOLDEN IMAGE OF MATCHLESS BEAUTY. THEN—

MOTHER! FATHER! I WILL MARRY BUT...

...ONLY ONE SUCH AS THIS!

IF YOU FIND A WOMAN AS BEAUTIFUL AS THIS IMAGE, I WILL MARRY HER.

WE WILL FIND HER. THIS IMAGE... WILL BE TAKEN... FROM TOWN TO TOWN ...TILL SUCH A GIRL IS FOUND.

YOU'LL NEVER FIND HER.

MONTHS ROLLED BY. THEN AT LAST ONE DAY —

THE MAIDEN IS FOUND, SIR— IN THE CITY OF SAGALA.

WHAT? CAN IT BE SO?

THE DELIGHTED OLD COUPLE SENT FORTH A MESSENGER WITH RICH GIFTS FOR THE MAIDEN AND HER PARENTS.

LET HER BE BROUGHT HERE WITH ALL SPEED.

KUMARA RECEIVED THE NEWS WITH MIXED FEELINGS.

WHEN I GOT THE STATUE MADE, I NEVER IMAGINED THAT SUCH A GIRL COULD BE FOUND.

BUT NOW THAT SHE IS FOUND, I CAN HARDLY WAIT TO SEE HER!

THEY SAY THAT COMPARED WITH THE IMAGE...

...SHE IS FAR, FAR LOVELIER! I CANNOT EVEN IMAGINE THE EXTENT OF HER BEAUTY!

HE IMPATIENTLY AWAITED THE ARRIVAL OF THE GIRL.

IS THAT HER CARRIAGE?

NO! IT IS NOT. OH, HOW SLOWLY THE HOURS CRAWL BY!

EACH PASSING DAY, THOUGHTS OF HER KEPT HIM COMPANY.

OH!

IT IS NIGHT ALREADY; THE TENTH NIGHT SINCE SHE SET OUT. WHERE IS SHE?

FATHER, MOTHER — SHE IS STILL NOT COME. WHAT COULD DELAY HER SO?

SHE... SHE MUST BE ON HER WAY, SON!

MOTHER, ARE YOU HIDING SOMETHING FROM ME? IS SOMETHING WRONG?

NOT AT ALL, SON.

HAVE THEY REFUSED THE PROPOSAL?

NO, MY SON.

THEN WHY HASN'T SHE COME YET? WHY? WHY?

WE MUST NOT KEEP IT FROM HIM ANY LONGER.

YES. HE WILL HAVE TO BE TOLD.

SON...

YES?

ARISE, YOUTHFUL ONE.

WHAT IS THIS SORROW THAT AFFLICTS YOU?

HOLY SIR, A WOMAN DIED ON THE ROAD AND...

...AND THE NEWS HAS FILLED ME WITH UNBEARABLE GRIEF.

SHE WAS THE MOST BEAUTIFUL WOMAN ON EARTH. SHE WAS THE WOMAN I WAS TO MARRY.

O KUMARA, YOU DO NOT GRIEVE BECAUSE A WOMAN DIED.

UN...?

YOU GRIEVE BECAUSE THE WOMAN YOU DESIRED DIED.

FROM DESIRE SPRINGS SORROW; FROM DESIRE SPRINGS FEAR. HE THAT IS FREE FROM DESIRE NEITHER SORROWS NOR FEARS.

AND KUMARA PROSTRATED HIMSELF BEFORE BUDDHA, AS THE TEACHER'S CALMNESS ENVELOPED HIS OWN HEART.

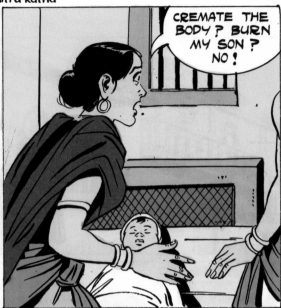

BUDDHA LOOKED AT THE CHILD AND SMILED.

THEN—

GO, FETCH ME A FEW MUSTARD SEEDS FROM A HOUSE THAT HAS NEVER KNOWN DEATH.

KRISHA GAUTAMI SET OUT ON HER QUEST.

TAK TAK

YES, WHAT IS IT?

MOTHER, CAN YOU GIVE ME A FEW MUSTARD SEEDS?

THE WOMAN WENT IN AND BROUGHT THE SEEDS.

HERE YOU ARE.

THANK YOU, MOTHER.

I TRUST THIS HOUSE HAS NEVER KNOWN DEATH.

WHAT ARE YOU SAYING, GOOD WOMAN?

WE THAT ARE LIVING ARE FEW, COMPARED WITH THOSE THAT HAVE DIED HERE.

THEN PLEASE TAKE BACK THESE MUSTARD SEEDS, FOR I HAVE NO USE FOR THEM.

KRISHA GAUTAMI WENT ON HER QUEST FROM HOUSE TO HOUSE, BUT EVERYWHERE IT WAS THE SAME. EVERY HOUSE HAD KNOWN DEATH AND EVERY DEAD BODY HAD BEEN BURNT TO ASHES.

...I LOST MY DAUGHTER...

...MY BROTHER DIED LAST YEAR...

THEY HAVE TAKEN MY OLD FATHER TO THE CREMATION GROUND TO BE BURNT...

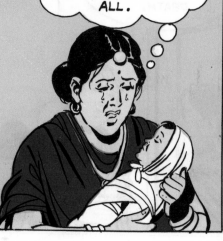

SO THOSE THAT ARE DEAD CAN NEVER BE CURED, AFTER ALL.

AH, WHAT A VAIN SEARCH WAS MINE!

KRISHA GAUTAMI WENT TO THE FOREST, LAID HER CHILD UPON A CARPET OF FALLEN LEAVES AND FLOWERS...

...AND THEN WENT BACK TO BUDDHA.

DID YOU GET THE MUSTARD SEEDS?

NO, HOLY SIR, I COULD NOT GET THEM. THERE IS NOT A HOUSE THAT HAS NOT KNOWN DEATH.

O KRISHA GAUTAMI, IT IS NOT YOU ALONE WHO HAVE LOST A CHILD TO DEATH.

I HAVE REALIZED THAT, O VENERABLE BUDDHA. ADMIT ME INTO YOUR ORDER.

I ACCEPT YOU, KRISHA GAUTAMI.

KRISHA GAUTAMI WAS ADMITTED INTO BUDDHA'S FOLD.

ONE DAY, WHEN IT WAS HER TURN, SHE LIT THE LAMP...

...AND SAT DOWN IN FRONT OF IT.

LIFE IS LIKE THESE FLAMES. SOME BURN ON; SOME FLICKER AND GO OUT.

KRISHA GAUTAMI CONTINUED TO MEDITATE WITH HER EYES FIXED ON THE FLAME OF THE LAMP...

...AND ATTAINED NIRVANA*.

* THE PERFECT STATE

# THE PERFECTIONIST

THERE WAS ONCE A CARPENTER WHO PRIDED HIMSELF ON THE QUALITY OF HIS WORK.

HMM-M. GOOD. BUT NOT GOOD ENOUGH. IT NEEDS IMPROVING. NOW LET ME SEE...

JUST THEN A MAN WALKED IN.

WHAT CAN I DO FOR YOU, SIR?

MY WIFE HAS BEEN BLESSED WITH A CHILD.

I NEED A CRADLE.

YOU HAVE COME TO THE RIGHT MAN. I'LL MAKE YOU THE BEST CRADLE YOU HAVE EVER SEEN.

A PERFECT DREAM.

WHEN CAN I COME FOR IT?

IT SHOULD BE READY IN A WEEK FROM NOW.

29

SOON THE CHILD WAS TOO OLD TO NEED A CRADLE, SO THE FATHER GAVE UP GOING TO THE CARPENTER.

BY AND BY THE BOY GREW UP, GOT MARRIED AND IN HIS TURN BECAME THE PROUD FATHER OF A CHILD.

GO TO OUR CARPENTER, TODAY.

ASK HIM IF THE CRADLE I HAD ORDERED FOR YOU IS READY. YOUR SON COULD USE IT.

SOON —

THE CRADLE MY FATHER ORDERED FOR ME WHEN I WAS BORN SHOULD BE READY BY NOW. SO...

IT ISN'T. AND LOOK, SIR!

LET ME MAKE ONE THING CLEAR. I TAKE PRIDE IN MY WORK.

AND I WILL NOT PERMIT YOU OR YOUR FATHER TO RUSH ME.

THE YOUNG MAN WAS ABOUT TO PROTEST BUT REALISED IT WOULD BE FUTILE TO ARGUE WITH THE PERFECTIONIST. SO HE QUIETLY LEFT THE PLACE.